THE
ETERNITY
PROPHECY

S. G. BASU

To placeholders, who, in lieu of little glory, keep order in the middle of chaos.

MIRACLE AT THE ORACLES' CONCLAVE

∞ IMPERIAL YEAR 20431∞

Excerpted from the account of Principal Scribe Ibn Karoujah, serving historian of the Empire of Veloressia, by appointment of His Divine Grace, the Adi Niappan of the six moons.

The Oracles' Conclave this year is a solemn affair. Although there are no victories to rejoice or conquests to celebrate, there are no losses to mourn either. And yet there is no peace.

There can be none. The Adi Niappan of our mighty Veloressian Empire, the supreme ruler chosen by the Gods, is 102 and dying, yet to this day, his successor has not been named.

For five years, the Imperial Council that holds power when the Adi Niappan is absent or undermined has been the de facto ruler of the Veloressian Empire. The Great Search – a holy quest to identify the Adi Niappan's successor – began five years ago. But time has flown by, and there is no indication of who the next Adi Niappan will be. It is an irregularity like no other. Never before has the search taken longer than two years.

Our world is whole while the Adi Niappan is living, but if he passes and his successor is not identified within a year of his passing, the Empire could crumble. The lengthy list of legal stipulations with the forty-nine protectorates that make up the Empire also includes one for secession. In the absence of an Adi Niappan, the protectorates are bestowed the right to break away.

It is no secret that the principal protectorates – those most wealthy and powerful – are no longer keen to be part of the Veloressian Empire. The only thread holding the Empire together is the Adi

Niappan's presence and the Oath of Allegiance the protectorates have sworn to him. Without the Adi Niappan, that thread will be broken. And what will the Empire be without its principal protectorates and the coinage that flows from them?

Then there is also the matter of the renegade protectorates, ones that, regardless of their lack of economic stature or self-sufficiency, clash openly with the Empire. The loudest among them is New Haphniss, clamoring against the Veloressian theocracy for decades. While the Haphnissians' protests have not amounted to much, their angst is spreading its dogged roots through the Empire, much like a chronic disease. Simply said, the situation is tenuous.

In the Veloressian Empire, the task of finding the Adi Niappan belongs to the Veloressian prophecy system, specifically its ten leading oracle clusters. But to their woe, in five years not one of the ten has produced a vision leading to the new Adi Niappan. Every year after the commencement of the Great Search, the Oracles' Conclave has met and departed with nothing but despair and shame in their hearts. This year seems to be no different.

It is the last hour of the Conclave, and 4,023 oracles from all major and minor oracle clusters are crammed in the expansive Imperial Chamber of Prophecies, their brows wrinkled as they discuss the onerous situation. Sighs rise in the air, swirling around the magnificent statuettes and extravagantly carved columns that ring the center of the chamber, reflecting off the ornately painted ceiling, and falling back heavily on the assembly again. Gentle murmurs grow into whispers and then into a restless humming. The assembly buzzes nonstop in a tiring, headache-inducing drone until the curtains part over center stage.

A Grand Niappan—a chief aide to the Adi Niappan—walks onstage, his black robe made resplendent with a wide red sash. He is followed by Sister Paramount Magetha, the leader of the Order of Divine Sight, a prominent cluster among the leading ten. Magetha rustles across the high podium, the edges of her silvery-white robe trailing behind her. Her cherubic face is flecked by the light and dark of the sacred fire burning below, and, even in the unreliable light, she can clearly be seen smiling.

It is odd that she should look so joyful in such grim circumstances, but not one of the 4,023 souls gathered at the conclave frowns, for Sister Paramount Magetha is not someone to be doubted. If she is smiling even when her elite coterie of oracles has not been able to spell out the name of the next Adi Niappan, then there has to be another reason for her smile, a reason the lesser people cannot fathom.

For over twenty thousand years, the Order of Divine Sight has prophesied without a glitch. They are the only oracle cluster of the Veloressian prophecy system with such a record. They have earned a reputation—a status, an honor—that is unshakable.

When Magetha walks across center stage, an expectant hush falls over the crowd. The Grand Niappan who ushered her in bows before scurrying away, leaving the elderly woman alone in the spotlight. Her voice, pleasing to hear yet forceful, rings clear even at the farthest rims of the assembly.

"On behalf of the Order of Divine Sight, I am honored to bring you most joyful news. We have humbly received the Eternity Prophecy all Veloressians have been praying for. We now know where we shall find the next Holy One."

She pauses, and as one moment stretches into another and then one more, the conclave stays silent. It is astounding how thousands of people can hold their breath at the same time. Then one oracle rises to his feet, as is custom when an Eternity Prophecy is announced. Then another rises, followed by one more, and another, the rustle of cloth echoing off the high dome of the Oracles' Conclave.

Magetha speaks when the entire assembly has stood. "His Holiness, the next Adi Niappan, will be found in New Haphniss, the blessed world with three stars."

A collective gasp rises through the chamber, defying long-practiced etiquette and forgetting decorum. Never before has an Adi Niappan been chosen from a pariah protectorate, one that has all but rejected the Veloressian theocracy.

Unfazed, Magetha smiles and bows at the assembly. Silvery gown swishing across the dark-grained, ancient wood floor, she disappears, specterlike, behind the bloodred curtains framing the podium.

1

Organized chaos is the most powerful political weapon of modern society.

—Adi Niappan of the three-star system

RUN

Oracle Prime Leon Courtee

Oracle Prime Leon Courtee hurried along the cobblestone pathway leading toward the Prophecy Archives. His feet, small and not used to walking, screamed for some rest, but Leon did not have time for such a luxury. He had to get away from the shadow that was following him.

He cast a quick glance backward, seeing nothing but the jubilant crowd thronging the plaza. Since Sister Paramount Magetha's announcement of the Eternity Prophecy at the Oracles' Conclave the previous night, Ajokkan, the Empire's expansive capital city, had erupted into festivities. On the other hand, Leon's life had spiraled toward a hell he had not even known existed.

His problem was simple: he alone knew Sister Paramount Magetha had lied about the Eternity Prophecy. He knew because he was the one who had received the true vision.

"Shouldn't have said a word last night," Leon muttered to himself, thinking of how the trouble had started with Magetha's announcement.

Shocked by Magetha's proclamation, Leon had decided to see her at the foundation right after the conclave ended. He had known confronting Magetha would be considered impudence. At the Order of Divine Sight, or the ODS, the sisterhood — charged with oversight of the organization even though not blessed with prescient minds themselves — was a tier above the oracles. They recruited and herded their flock of visionaries with the benevolence of egg farmers tending their fowl.

Since being drafted into the ODS as an oracle when he was sixteen, Leon had learned one important fact: defying the sisterhood was a serious step and a career-risking one. But Leon had not let the hesitation spread its root inside him. Wrapping his thickest *Pamisha* around himself as a shield against the chilly air, Leon had set across the wide grounds that lay between his quarters and the Sister Paramount's chambers. In part due to the postprophecy frenzy at the ODS, Leon had had to wait long for his chance at an audience with Magetha, but he was determined.

"You misread my vision," he had alleged, breathing in deep on seeing Magetha's eyes harden. "I never saw a boy in New Haphniss. I never saw a boy at all."

"Maybe it's not *your* vision I spoke about." Sister Magetha had strolled away, turning her back on him.

"That cannot be," Leon had protested. "I know none of our other oracles saw anything. I checked. I was the only one who — "

Magetha had walked over to touch his forehead with three fingers, and a tingle had spread throughout his body, calming his thoughts, relaxing his muscles as she gently tapped his forehead.

"Leon," she had said, "I know what I'm doing. Tonight at the conclave I announced what the Gods demanded of me. Your task, as my oracle prime, is to help me complete this work of the Gods. That, I want you to remember. Everything else you need to forget. Will you do that?"

Just like a puppet on a string, Leon had nodded. He had retired content and at peace.

That would have been it for a regular person, but Leon Courtee was no ordinary man. He was an oracle, a seer, a clairvoyant. Mind control did not hold him down for long. As soon as he opened his eyes that morning, he had remembered everything. It had not taken him long to realize that Magetha was trying to keep him quiet, which disturbed any little peace he had left.

Agitated, Leon had decided to find someone to confide in. He did not know for sure if anyone at the foundation could be trusted, but his hopes had quickly settled on one person. If there was a chance that someone would stand up for the truth, it had to be Sister Subordinate

Xihin, the seemingly frail, dark-eyed recent recruit of the Order. Not too long ago she had supported Leon, much to the chagrin of Sister Paramount Magetha. The issue then — oracles occasionally straying from the guidelines of quarantine while working on a vision — had not been too serious, but it was not entirely trivial either. Magetha had waved it away, but Xihin had fought for stringent enforcement until Magetha ceded. Xihin, Leon knew, could be one with advice on his current quandary.

Once again Leon had made the trip across the courtyard, this time with the suns beating down on him. Leon had trudged along, forcing his feet forward, chanting a prayer hymn over and over so he'd not utter a profanity. *Remember your station*, Leon reminded himself, but the frustration kept bubbling up. Did the ODS need to be so large? Or designed like a penitentiary? He knew that was the way things were at every cluster. But did it have to be?

Each oracle cluster, particularly the leading ten in the Empire, owned foundations — expansive compounds where their oracles lived. Replete with every material need, they were cloistered havens for the oracles. The seers were not held captive, but they were urged to stay away from the world outside the foundation, from the distractions and noises that could mar their tender sensibilities.

The foundation buildings of the Order of Divine Sight were arranged in the form of a ringed fortress. The outermost, administrative ring was separated by a sizable band of open ground from the next ring, which housed the living quarters of the sisterhood. Next, separated by another strip of open land, were the accommodations for the oracles. At the very center were the vision chambers where the oracles held their daily foresight sessions and attempted a glimpse into the distant.

It had taken Leon the better part of an hour to reach Xihin's office, but as fate would have it, Xihin had already left for her routine morning walk across the city. Leon had paced her empty office for a bit, finally deciding to leave a note. Scribbling hastily on a small piece of parchment, he had placed it far inside one of her bureau drawers.

That would have been a good time to abandon his quest for truth and to pursue his usual routine, but did he? No.

Almost right away, he had thought of checking the Prophecy Archives — the central place where every oracle's visions were recorded and stored. All of the oracle clusters had a direct feed, a superhighway of information that linked their vision chambers to the storage clocks of the archives. Every prophecy made by the oracles was routed there instantly and, after the head of the cluster validated it, stored for perpetuity. The archives had to have information about his newest vision, Leon had deduced. He needed to find it and extract a copy before he could challenge Magetha again.

With that plan in mind, Leon had headed out of the foundation. Now, as Leon neared the Archives, the dual suns were approaching their peak, their intense white rays scorching. Leon's spine tingled when he was a hundred paces away from the Archive's vaulted entrance. His feet slowed and his shoulders tightened as he felt a gaze burn into his back.

Someone was watching, Leon was sure.

Leon stopped, his heart thrashing wildly inside his chest. Did Magetha know he had slipped out of the foundation? Had she sent someone after him? He had defied her order to forget about the incorrect prophecy. She would be furious, perhaps banish him from the ODS.

Leon looked up at the towering facade of the Prophecy Archives and hesitated. There was still time; he could still turn away and forget about it.

Leon's fist clenched at the thought of surrender. No, he could not simply forget. This was not just an everyday prophecy of the upcoming year's weather pattern, but the holiest of them all — the Eternity Prophecy. He could not knowingly forsake its sanctity. Banishment from the ODS he could endure, but not living with the knowledge that the Eternity Prophecy had been read wrongly and he had done nothing to correct it.

He glanced around once more, hoping to detect the person trailing him but found nothing out of the ordinary. All he saw was the commonplace crowd of townsfolk going about their usual business, a few excited sightseers. He shook off the unsettling feeling and hurried inside. He did not have much time.

The Prophecy Archives was a public building with a bleak, gray stone facade and a cavernous inside that stretched out like a maze around the central portico. Clerks—all old, crusty women—sat like hawks at the entryway. They questioned every visitor, often for a long time, before they admitted anyone inside. For a public building, the Prophecy Archives and its contents were very closely guarded.

Leon did not have any trouble with the clerks, who knew him well enough to let him pass into the inner galleries. All Leon needed was a search portal where he could look for his vision. Once in the portals room, he located a station—a gray, bowl-shaped machine with a dusty, oblong screen, that rested on stubby legs and ponderous feet. The station was in the back, tucked away from the three other occupied stations, but not too far in the shadows. Casting a quick, wary look around, Leon entered the information he was seeking.

The portal turned into a rotating orb of light, as was customary when a search was being conducted, and then beeped.

"Invalid entry," the screen informed coldly.

Leon stiffened. Was he entering the correct details? He paused and pulled his hands away from the screen. Closing his eyes, Leon recalled the day he had had the vision. It came back to him quickly.

Visions were precious. They did not happen often. Day after day, oracles sat through foresight sessions seeking a path to view unseen times. Most days, they wound up staring blankly at the curved glass walls of the vision chamber. Some days though, they were blessed with a sight. No oracle, not any Leon knew of anyway, forgot any of their visions. Since discovering his gift when he was ten, Leon had seen quite a few. And he still remembered each of them clearly.

While every vision was important, Leon's last was remarkable, a blessing from the God of Sight himself. He had seen the next Adi Niappan. He had finally become what every oracle dreamed of being—a true prophet. And now . . .

He *had* to find the vision. Frowning, Leon entered the details again: his name, the date of the vision, the place.

The orb spun on the screen for a bit and then, once again, "Invalid entry" flashed brightly.

"No, no," Leon muttered, shaking his head as he entered the details the third time, checking and rechecking his entry before starting the search.

Nothing changed. The same words, "Invalid entry," mocked him one more time.

It was gone. The record of his vision, the proof of his exemplary work, had been removed. Tiredness creeped up his bones and his body felt heavy, as if he had not slept in days.

Leon could hardly think anymore. By the Imperial Laws of Data Integrity, deletion of public records—or modifying them—was a crime punishable by a life term in prison. And deleting a record from the Prophecy Archives? That was unthinkable. Yet, someone had done just that. Who could have done such a thing? Was it Sister Paramount Magetha? But why would she do it?

Up until then, Leon had thought Magetha had made a mistake and was simply reluctant to admit it. But now it seemed like a willful falsehood. Only, he did not know why she'd lie.

Leon fell back and rested his head against the arched back of the chair. Drained of the strength to even keep his eyes open, he let his spent lids droop and let his thoughts float free.

The vision had taken a long time to come to him. It was strange that not one oracle had been able to catch a glimpse of the next Adi Niappan for such a long time. Strange it had seemed to him too, until he saw what he saw.

He saw a girl.

They had been looking for a boy, just like they were expected to. The Adi Niappans were always found as a boy aged three or four, with numerous siblings, and always a child from a tightly knit, happy family.

This one was an aberration on all counts. First, it was a doe-eyed, curly haired, dusky-skinned girl. She was about four years of age, but, second, she had just one brother. Third, there was no happy family around her. Her father's pale, steely eyes glinted with wickedness while the mother and children cowered in fear around him. They lived on an underdeveloped, dusty, and barren planet; Leon had not seen it clearly enough to figure out which. Leon caught a hint of nervousness in her; it was odd how a child so young looked over her shoulder ever so often, as if she were always on the lookout for some unknown danger. The halo of divinity danced over her head though. It cast a soft glow on her eyes, giving her the kind of piteous look that came upon a cornered animal staring at its ruin. It was a heartbreaking picture of the most sought-after person in the Empire.

That was all he had seen.

Leon sat up and, cradling his head in his palms, thought furiously. *Why didn't Magetha announce my vision at the conclave?* Was it because someone else had seen a conflicting vision?

No, he pushed the idea away. He was Oracle Prime, the lead prescient at the Order of Divine Sight. Leon knew the obligations handed to the lesser oracles, and he kept track of their outcomes. He would know if anyone within the Order had seen anything about the Adi Niappan.

Leon decided to check the archives again. Magetha would not have announced the Eternity prophecy — the most fundamental and awaited vision in the Empire — without making sure the archives had a matching entry. Leon wondered who had seen the version Magetha announced at the conclave, and what they had seen.

The portal accepted his entry and, after the requisite spinning of the orb, it spat out a page-long description of the newest Eternity

Prophecy. Predictably, it matched what Magetha had said at the conclave. Leon's eyes did not dwell on the central matter; he rushed to the end and on the name of the person cited as the receiver of the vision.

Oracle Junior Ainer Ahloi.

"Impossible," Leon whispered, his fists clenching. Leon Courtee was Oracle Prime for a reason—he knew everything that was to be known about prescience. He also knew each man and woman who worked under him, even the junior oracles. Ainer was not ready for a vision of this scale; he would not be ready for a few more years.

This was a sham. This was planted so Magetha could make her claim. But why?

Leon's mind squirmed, a million thoughts tangled together in an unholy mess. He needed to speak to someone who could help investigate this, someone who had the reach, the brains, and the brawn.

Mako!

His ex-neighbor's son Mako was in the Special Ops unit of the Imperial Intelligence Bureau. He also offered casual investigative services to private parties, especially when tempted with the right price or a suitable challenge. Besides, Mako had known him for too long to refuse him help.

A voice—his years of wisdom and practical sense speaking in unison—in Leon's head told him to go back to the foundation. It was getting late for his foresight session, and Leon Courtee was never late. People would be suspicious if he went missing for too long.

But he had to locate Mako or at least pass him a message.

Sister Paramount Magetha wouldn't be happy if she found out, the voice cautioned.

Leon did not care. He needed to find out why his vision was missing. He had to reach Mako before getting back to the foundation.

Closing the portal off, Leon hurried out of the building and shuffled toward the northeast end of the plaza. Leon knew where

Mako lived but he did not head that way. Instead he strode in the opposite direction, toward an alehouse that Mako often visited. Not only was the place far closer than Mako's house, but since Leon often met Mako at the alehouse he could leave a note there without attracting too much attention.

He picked the shortest route across, one that cut through the abandoned tannery rows and would save him time. Cherishing the quietness, Leon walked determinedly along the alleyway. Within a few steps, he reached the tannery rows. There were houses all around, their fractured walls gaping at him, but there was not a soul in sight.

He had left the humdrum of the plaza far behind when he felt the gaze again. This time Leon did not look around; even the idea of looking terrified him for some reason. He rushed a little more, forcing his feet to step quicker.

As soon as Leon turned around a dead tree near the old tannery, he saw the man. He was quickly drawing near along the cross street, and the cybernetic implants on his head glinted menacingly in the sunlight when the oversize hood of his brown overalls slipped off. His face, as much as Leon could see from the distance, was uneven, like lumpy bread baked by a child. Parts of it—the left side mostly— seemed missing. Never had Leon seen anything so grotesque. He wanted to scream, but his throat was frozen along with his heart.

The man kept approaching as Leon stared, open-mouthed. There was an odd, casual stealth about the man, as if he was an apparition who had floated out of the netherworld. He was about twenty steps away when Leon sensed malice in the air. An unholy fear washed over him, leaving every hair on his body tingling. Evil, its eyes dark and penetrating, stared coldly at his soul. Leon did not know why, but he knew he could not let the man catch up to him. For a moment, Leon forgot to breathe or run or walk. Then, as if he was waking up from a dream, Leon tottered backward and hurried back toward the plaza.

Tip, tap. Tip, tap. The footsteps, inching closer, were light and unnatural in their rhythmic perfection. They made Leon think of death and . . . darkness.

Tip, tap. Tip, tap.

Leon's trembling feet rushed to cover the never-ending distance to the plaza.

Tip, tap. Tip, tap.

Running is of no use, Leon thought, wiping the sweat off his forehead. He could not give up either. This had to be Magetha's conspiracy. She was trying to stop him, obliterate his vision and obliterate him. He could not let that happen. He would not let her win. There had to be a way to fight back. There had to be something.

The hum of the crowd reached his ears. The plaza was getting closer. There was a chance, he thought, that he could get away. Surrounded by a crowd, he would be safe.

But what if he could not get away? He had to take precautions. But how? The only way was transference — pushing the memory of his vision telepathically to someone. But even if he broadcast a thought, receiving it was not something just anyone could do. Commoners or ordinary people did not recognize a thought stream like an oracle could, so here, far from the ODS, there was little chance of it succeeding.

Still, Leon prepared. Focusing his thoughts on the transference protocol, Leon broke into an unstable run. If he could find someone, anyone, he would push the message.

He knew he'd possibly fail. He had never transferred to a commoner, no one had in hundreds of years. Transference to ordinary citizens had long been prohibited by Imperial law, but Leon cared little about the law just then. He would have to try.

But first he had to find someone.

Tinkling footsteps dashed toward him, closer and closer . . . His left side burned, a pulled muscle. He hobbled forward, faster, his feet feeling foreign under him, his breathing ragged . . .

Leon looked around frantically for someone, anyone who could receive his thoughts. He saw no one. Only row upon row of dilapidated buildings boarded up and long abandoned.

Footsteps rushed close . . . closer still . . .

A steel arm wrapped around his throat. Leon gasped for air, clawing frantically to loosen the chokehold. His feet thrashed against the pavement in a futile attempt to break free. A long sabre held in beat-up metal fingers slashed across Leon's abdomen before he could turn around and look at the man's face.

A white-hot pain erupted, shooting upward through Leon's body as he fell forward. He clutched at his belly and warm wetness spilled over his hands.

Blood. And a mass of dimply softness . . . his insides.

The stones paving the road rushed up to meet Leon as he gasped for breath.

Specks of black dotted his sight, and he saw the girl again, the halo of divinity still swirling above her head. Her curly mane was pulled away from her face and tied into a knot at the back. Her hands gripped her stomach as if trying to suppress a pain. "Eos!" someone called, and she turned to look. Even in the pale light that barely lit her face, Leon saw the dark mark . . . an old scar shaped like a crescent moon . . . across her forehead.

He had to tell someone this . . . the name . . . the mark . . . someone . . . anyone . . .

Something sharp and cold pushed through his ribs and into his heart, retreating as rapidly as it had entered his body. Pain exploded from his back and spread through him in a hot, piercing wave. Warmth flooded his throat and gurgled into his mouth.

Just before the world started to fade to black, Oracle Prime Leon Courtee saw the strangest pair of eyes — irises so pale that you would not think they existed — staring at him through the cracks of a boarded-up window. Leon's waning senses stumbled in the murkiness that was falling swiftly across his mind, desperate to initiate the transference procedure.

HOPE

Noell Rivans

The unending city lights of Ajokkan, stretching like a jewel-encrusted blanket all the way to horizon, almost blinded Noell as the airship circled around for landing. She looked away from the window of the cargo transporter, shielding her eyes from the glare. It was the biggest and brightest city she had ever seen, and the sight made her heart flutter nervously.

"We will be landing soon. Prepare for touchdown." A mechanical voice spread throughout the cramped hold of the airship, and about twenty people who had been huddled in small groups in between the piles of boxes, sacks, and packages stirred uneasily.

Noell pulled her half-asleep daughter close and, clutching her infant son tighter to her bosom, she shuffled nearer to the two large wooden crates that provided some sort of stability. They also cast much-needed shadows over their faces and obscured the little their veils could not cover.

She had never been anywhere on her own, let alone to a place as far away as this. If someone had told her a month ago that she would someday visit Ajokkan, the capital of the Empire of the Twenty-Three Stars, the seat of the mighty Veloressians, she would have laughed the idea away. Now it sprawled below her, as far as her eyes could see, in an unbelievable spectacle. Noell gulped a few times, but the dryness in her throat refused to go away.

In Milokan, where she grew up, Noell had never walked beyond the mud walls that circled their home. She was not allowed to; she was too valuable. What if she slipped and fell and got a scar on her precious face?

Noell was born beautiful. With rare amber eyes and even rarer auburn hair that curled naturally, she would have been treasured in any household. To her needy family, being the only daughter after four sons, she was a god-sent gift. Her parents taught her to be timid and docile, just the way men on Milokan wanted their women. For sixteen years, her parents raised her in every luxury they could afford so she could fetch them the largest dowry offering at her debut.

Noell did not disappoint. Her dowry was enough to cover the farmland her parents had always coveted and to leave her brothers enough to look for wives themselves.

On the night of her wedding, her mother had said, "You're a lucky girl, Noell." Her mother had kissed her forehead as she wrapped her in the long folds of Milokanese bridal attire. The fabric was heavy and itchy, and Noell had gasped for air as more adornments were piled on her. "The richest man in the Robben-Xiu System has chosen you as his bride. I'm so proud of you."

Noell still remembered her mother's suffocating embrace, her weather-beaten, weary face crinkled into a happy smile. Noell wanted to be happy, but she was not so sure about her luck. Luca Daksson, the man who had won her hand, was almost twenty years older than she was. He was the owner of the largest legume farm in the system and rich enough to hire a private airship to the wedding and back. She had to admit he was good-looking—dark skinned, pale eyed, and a confident smile that made her sixteen-year-old heart flutter a little. Yet there was something odd about him, something out of place. And then, his home was on 4217, the third planet in the Robben-Xiu System—a dry, dusty hellhole. It was two-day journey from her own 4210, a distance Noell found unimaginable.

"Mama." Her daughter's soft voice made Noell turn away from the hypnotic spread of lights outside and from the memories crowding her head. "Are we close?"

"Yes, Eos. We are."

"Mama," the tiny voice chided. "You can't call me by my real name, remember?"

Noell ran a caressing palm over her daughter's veiled head and sighed. She spoke like a child much older than her four years. No, she spoke almost like a grown-up. So wise, so calm . . . not a trace of childhood left in her . . . all because of that monster of a father. She had seen as much violence in four years as some people see in their entire lifetimes. Eos had learned to survive hell, but she paid a hefty price—her innocence. Noell clutched her child tighter. Her eyes lingered on the crescent-shaped scar on Eos's forehead and a tight lump grew bigger in her throat.

"Yes," Noell replied, stifling a sigh and blinking to drive away the stinging tears. "You're Aidah now."

Little hands circled Noell's waist and a head pressed against her side comfortingly. "You worry too much, Mama. Don't worry. We will be fine. I know."

Noell pulled her daughter closer and smiled, taking care to keep her ice-cold palms a secret so they would not scare the child. The children had endured plenty—sneaking out of the house in the middle of the night with just a bagful of food and barely enough money to secure a passage to Ajokkan, and that too on a freighter ship that treated its human passengers no different from its cargo—in the last two days. It had been harrowing enough.

Noell's sight blurred as the cargo transporter sunk lower, her heart beating faster and louder. At least they had made it to Ajokkan safely. She knew her odds frighteningly well, and they were not good. It would not be long before Luca realized she was in Ajokkan, and then he would come looking. All she could hope to do was make good use of this head start.

***

The Waterside Alehouse was a misshapen stone structure near a small lake. The area around it could be called bleak, if not desolate. An abandoned tannery stood next to it, casting dark, dilapidated shadows around. The alehouse was barely a few hundred paces away from the big, lively plaza around the Prophecy Archives, yet it felt so far removed from the humdrum, like it was a world away.

Noell stared at the tavern's huge stone pillars and old hardwood door. The door was closed, but she could hear sounds of merrymaking wafting out from inside. It was unexpected that a shop in these ruined quarters would be open at all, yet this one bustled with activity. A large crowd was gathered inside, their outlines illuminated in the stained-glass windows.

Perfect place for us, Noell thought as she stared at the lonely locale. Clutching her children tightly, she took a cautious step forward, and then another, until she had found shelter in the shadows of the alehouse.

CALL

Mako Nuyin

Mako Nuyin leaned against the dark, wood-paneled door of the Waterside Alehouse and pushed it open. The warmth inside caressed his face as soon as the doors parted; the aroma of cooked meats drifted through the room, its spiciness no doubt a little heavy-handed for his taste, but it roused his appetite in an instant.

As was his habit, Mako quickly scanned the room before he stepped inside. The alehouse was busy, as expected, with crocks of frothy drinks strewn across every table. It was mostly full of shoddily dressed men, their weather-beaten, craggy faces stretched into placid smiles as they banded around the tables.

Nothing was out of place.

Mako's gaze drifted to the long counter across the back where Arum, the wizened alemaster with a shock of green hair, held his court. His brews were the reason why Mako visited this broken-down dump of a place over and over again. Arum's excellent ales, the best that money could buy in Ajokkan, justified the long, meandering walk through the tumbledown tannery rows.

Arum, busily pouring and mixing drinks, waved. Despite the crowd and his usual steady business, he had seen Mako walk in. That was the other reason Mako liked visiting: Arum, the charming alemaster with an endless bounty of anecdotes, also had the most efficient and affable service in Ajokkan.

Mako weaved through the crowd of sweaty-smelling men to a seat at the counter. A foaming jug of his favorite bitter, Dead Mutt, was already waiting. Mako sighed, his hand wrapping eagerly around the cool handle of the mug.

What a perfect way to end a day like this!

He had taken a few sips of the Dead Mutt when Arum strolled

closer to his end.

"Busy day, Mako?" the alemaster asked, leaning over the counter, all the while looking away from his face.

"Very," Mako replied, keeping his voice guarded. "Good times, my friend."

"Hmm," Arum said. He pulled a few bottles off the shelf behind him and mixed a colorful concoction in a fancy glass cup. "War it is, then?"

Mako took another swig. "Obviously. Everyone knows New Haphniss would never agree to the prophecy. They would fight until death."

Yesterday's Eternity Prophecy, with its claim that New Haphniss was the birthplace of the new Adi Niappan, had stirred up more trouble than usual. The protectorate of New Haphniss had been opposed to the Empire for years, clinging on pointlessly to an obsolete form of government called democracy. New Haphniss had never been an important planet, it was not rich in minerals and it was not a cultural bastion either. But their constant protests had the Empire's attention. Their tireless dissension undermined the absoluteness of the Empire's control, opening the path for other protectorates to get similar ideas. What if everyone rose up in revolt? What then? New Haphniss was the biggest thorn in the Empire's side, had been so for years.

The new Eternity Prophecy had stirred the simmering pot of tensions and flung it up in the air. It had stripped the veil off the conflict and exposed the bruising hostilities. It had left New Haphniss in a quandary. If they acceded to the claim of the prophecy, it would mean accepting the Empire's theocratic tenets. But that was not likely. Given how New Haphniss was staunchly against the theocracy, they would never stoop to legitimizing the claim. So to secure its Adi Niappan from New Haphniss, the Empire had a single recourse: to extract him by force. War with New Haphniss was inevitable.

War is good, Mako thought as he emptied his mug. *War means new business and a whole lot of money. Everything is looking up.*

Arum had walked away to the other end of the counter. Now he sauntered back and topped off Mako's drink. "You must've been summoned?" he asked.

Mako nodded. He would not miss being part of the war efforts for the universe. Wars were when fortunes were made and lives of the truly clever changed for the better. The best time for Special Ops agents like him was now, when spies were in demand and everyone, from groups trying to thwart war to people trying to incite it, needed him. Now was when he would be openly flattered and his services bid upon.

Arum leaned on the counter, his lustrous eyes intent. "Leaving soon?"

"In two days," Mako replied. He had gotten some of the highest bids, and the task he was assigned was flagged a top priority. "Been asked to locate a key player."

"Your father will be happy," Arum commented. "If war breaks out, which it most definitely will, you'll be in the war zone, just like the Armed Forces."

The ale suddenly tasted far too bitter, making Mako's face twist into a grimace. Warzone or not, Father would never be happy. In his eyes, Mako would always remain a wasted opportunity. Mako earned twice as much as he would have had he pursued his father's dreams for him — becoming an Imperial soldier. But that did not make a difference to his father.

Perhaps too much intelligence was not a good thing after all. Mako had always been ahead of his peers — in academics, in physicals, and even in the drastically difficult socials. It was only natural that a man of his abilities would end up in the Imperial Services. Mako could have chosen any branch of service; his evaluation score guaranteed him a place regardless of his choice. Mako chose the Intelligence Bureau over the glamorous Diplomatic Services or the glorified Armed Forces. The reason was simple — the IB paid more handsomely than the others. His father did not speak to Mako for a year after he had made his choice.

"I'm not going to the war zone. I'm being sent to Robben-Xiu." The words churned his guts on their way out. Mako had hoped for an assignment to New Haphniss, but that did not happen. At least the money was just as good.

"Robben-Xiu?" Arum balked. "That's the other end of the galaxy. Why are they sending you there?"

Mako wished he knew. All he was given were the coordinates of the package "bioreactor" he had to retrieve. Such ambiguity was norm in the Imperial Intelligence Bureau. They liked to play their hand close, and reveals, even to its own agents, often came at the last moment.

Arum reached out and patted his shoulder. "That's all right. I'm sure they're paying you well," he said. "That's all that matters."

Mako chuckled. Arum understood him better than his headstrong, old-fashioned father. He emptied the mug in one long gulp.

"I should get going," he said, handing Arum a wad of money.

"So soon?"

"Yes, need to prepare for the trip," Mako replied.

"Listen . . ." Arum's voice faded. He stood there as if in a trance, his gaze skimming the burnished surface of the counters. Something was bothering the man.

Mako cleared his throat.

"Um . . ." Arum was clearly hesitating. Had it been any other person, Mako would have not spared another glance or a word. His time and advice did not come cheap, and Mako did not go about wasting them on random people. But this was Arum.

"What is it?" Mako prodded.

Arum ran a hand through his forest-green hair before looking up; his always-luminous eyes had a patina of worry over them. "Can you meet me out back?" he said in a rushed whisper.

The request was odd; the way Arum's gaze darted nervously across the room as he waited for Mako's reply was odder still.

"Of course," Mako said. He walked out of the alehouse, a frown deeply etched on his forehead.

***

The back of the alehouse was a mess. Two large trash vats lined the sides, the stench from them not strong enough to make Mako retch, yet its presence forceful. There were other piles, stacks of broken-down equipment, furniture, building material, and whatnots. Coarse rubble lined a narrow path through the clutter that led up to a worn-out, paint-stripped door.

Mako treaded softly along the path, his feet buoyant from the ale, his gaze a little imprecise. The lit windows of living quarters atop the alehouse drew his attention as he walked.

The owner of the alehouse kept a few helping hands here, according to Arum. The panes were drawn so he could not see the people inside, but shadows flittered back and forth across the room.

What a place to live.

Just before the back door opened and Arum stumbled out, Mako caught the glimpse of a silhouette in the window, and then the lights went out. Mako frowned.

Did I just see a woman?

"Sorry," Arum apologized. "I won't hold you for very long."

Mako's eyes were still stuck on the window. "Is there a woman up there?"

Arum waved away his question. "A woman? You didn't have *that* much to drink tonight." He chuckled loudly.

"I thought . . ." Mako let his words trail off. He was pretty sure he'd seen a woman. But it did not make sense. No respectable woman would live atop a rundown alehouse. Besides, why would Arum lie to him? He looked away from the window and scanned Arum's face.

The man looked a little pale. "What did you need?"

Arum cast a quick glance around and shuffled closer to Mako. "Remember Roli?" he whispered.

Mako had to think for a moment. He recalled the vague image of a scruffy boy with matted gray hair and weird white eyes. An orphan squatter in the tannery rows, Roli often ran errands for the alehouse. Once, Arum had sent Roli to deliver a crate of Dead Mutt to Mako's house. The boy had skillfully negotiated a hefty tip.

"Yes," Mako replied, smiling at the memory. "What about him?"

"He came by this afternoon." Arum's gaze scooted around the darkness. "The boy was shaking all over, like he'd seen a ghost. You know how Roli is . . . nothing rattles him. But, today — "

"Did he tell you what was bothering him?" Mako asked, unsure why Arum was telling him this.

"Well . . . I don't know if I should . . . He . . ."

Mako tried to remain patient, but it was getting difficult to put up with the dawdling. In two days he had to leave for a fringe system on a mission. There was packing to do, a strategy to make, research to complete. Arum was taking too damn long. Even the light-headedness from the Dead Mutt was starting to clear.

Mako shook his head. "Arum, you called me here to tell me about this, didn't you? So tell me already," he said irritably.

Arum clutched him and pulled him near. "Roli said . . . he'd seen a murder . . . of . . . an oracle."

The man has lost it, Mako thought.

Oracles were the spokes in the wheel of the prophecy system that drove the Veloressian theocracy, and they were held above most things in this world. Oracles did not get murdered just like that. In the Empire, oracles did not get murdered — ever. If such an unfortunate thing were to happen, all hell would break loose and Ajokkan would be on the highest alert. Yet . . . all was usual. Not even the news of a missing oracle.

Mako was close to laughing it away, but the look on Arum's face gave him pause. The man's dark, wide, and restless gaze, the almost unnoticeable tremble of his lips, his bony fingers that dug into Mako's arm as if it was the plank keeping him afloat—everything was out of place for the Arum he knew.

A tiny chill tingled his spine and sped upward.

Could it be true? Had the boy really seen the murder of an oracle?

SEARCH

Bryanna Tu-Fei

From the window of her cluttered attic, Bryanna watched the darkness of night rolling into Ajokkan. She was waiting for the right moment to leave for her late-night shift at the Cognitivus, the digital data-processing center of the Veloressian Empire where she worked as a data organizer, or DO.

Ten-year-old Nico lay in her lap, purring contentedly as Bryanna rubbed his belly. Felines, so Bryanna believed, were nature's best attempt at perfection. Their beauty, their heartwarming mannerisms, their sass — Bryanna admired it all. Mostly, she admired their resilience. Each one of her cats, from the hairless Sin-Lomor to the shaggy Miskadoon, and every other breed in between, inspired her. For starters, they kept Bryanna alive. They also kept her going, wanting to fight, and hoping to get justice for Kianto.

Ten years ago, when Kianto died in her arms, she had lost her will to live. What was the point? What did she have to look forward to? Her only son — the one hope she had clung to after the untimely passing of her beloved husband — was gone, along with the dreams of a future, of grandchildren. It had always been the two of them, mother and son together, braving a future of uncertainty after Kianto's father died of renal failure and resulting complications. Kianto had only been a year old then, and raising him was the one thing that drove her forward. With Kianto gone, Bryanna lost the will to carry on.

After putting Kianto to eternal rest — a full honor event at the Order of Divine Sight where he had been a valued apprentice to the sisterhood — Bryanna had thought of ways to kill herself. She had stared at the kitchen knives, tested out sailor's ropes, researched flammable fluids. But in the end, she could not find the nerve to do it. She had no choice but to live on, knowing nothing she did mattered anymore. The thought that no one would even blink if she were gone tormented her. Each day, she wrangled with the pain—a pain that slowly ate away her heart and turned all her hair gray.

Then she discovered a smoker's den two houses away, where addicts met to share drugged smokepots. She took to the smoke like a bird took to the skies, welcoming it into her soul, releasing herself into its endlessness. A whole week passed without her realizing it. When Bryanna had come out of the swirling, rainbow-hued mists, she knew that was the way to exist until death released her.

Two days later, Nico had appeared at her doorstep.

She was on her way to the smoker's den to secure another week of oblivion when she had come across the mewling bundle that was Nico. Soaked to his bones, the barely month-old kitten had come up her stairs seeking shelter from the pooling rain. For a long while, Bryanna looked for his mother or siblings, but found neither. Maybe they had been washed away by the rains or killed by a streetcar. Who knew?

Nico stayed. And Bryanna never got a chance to get back to the smoker's den. The kitten needed her, and Bryanna was ready to give it everything she had. By the time Nico got better, Bryanna had opened her heart and home to two more cats. It grew from there.

"And then there were twenty," Bryanna whispered, twiddling Nico's ears. Outside her attic window, the world was lighting up as darkness of night grew thicker. Neon lights hanging above the shops across the street seemed to try their best to lure in passersby. Some stopped to lounge, other people—mostly men and women returning from the day's work—busily walked by. The city was starting to glow with its night light. All was well in Ajokkan.

Bryanna leaned to reach a rickety table next to her couch, taking care to not upset Nico's repose, and grabbed a thick, brown folder. The folder had a tired look to it—the cover had cracked in places and had collected copious smudges over the years. Bryanna ran an affectionate finger over its worn-out surface. Just like Nico, this too had been her companion and confidante since Kianto passed — and a witness to her growing courage.

"Mom is a brave old woman, isn't she, Nico?" Bryanna crooned, scratching the cat's neck.

Ten years ago, she would not have dreamed of having enough strength to scrutinize the circumstances surrounding Kianto's death. Call it a mother's instinct, call it a hunch, but Bryanna had known that something was odd about Kianto's death from the start. How could a healthy man in his prime with no apparent illness die coughing up blood? Even the family medic had frowned, but he did not dare question the medic of the ODS, who had cited viral infection as cause. Nor did Bryanna, at the time. Questioning the ODS and their report on Kianto's death was unthinkable. The oracle clusters were divinity, obviously less so than the Gods, the Adi Niappan, and the Grand Niappans — in that specific order — but divine nonetheless. And in the Empire, questioning such divinity was the last thing that came to anyone's mind. Yet . . . that niggling doubt stayed like a grain of sand in her shoe.

Later, Bryanna knew. It took a few years, but Bryanna was convinced Kianto's death was not natural. Bryanna also knew that she would get her son justice somehow.

Bryanna scratched Nico's flaccid belly, making him purr again. "All because of you," she said. She sat quietly for a while, grateful for Nico's presence, grateful that his arrival had given her a new lease on life. Then, gently putting him down on the couch, Bryanna headed out.

Icy-cold droplets of rain stabbed at Bryanna's puffy face as she plodded down her front stairs. She looked upward, her eyes scanning the clouds above.

Nothing fearsome, she thought to herself. *Just a drizzle and it'll pass.*

Bryanna straightened at the bottom of the stairs, rubbing her right hip slightly. Then, with a bracing breath, she slogged forward.

The Cognitivus headquarters were right around the corner from where she lived. All her life, up until Kianto passed, Bryanna had been a teacher. Kianto's death took her out of everything—living, hoping, and finally teaching. When she got her life back together, she considered going back to the things she had known before and loved, until she realized she couldn't. The Imperial Education Services considered her unsuitable to be near children. Decades of unparalleled service was wiped out, just like that, due to a few months of intoxicated haze. Bryanna kept looking. She had to find a job, for Nico.

Never had she thought of being somewhere like the Cognitivus, which seemed to be made for the young. Kids barely out of their teens started as apprentices and continued working at Cognitivus until they grew too old—about thirty, Bryanna guessed—to fit in with the young crowd. Everything was fresh at the company, other than a few grayed-and-old exceptions with outstanding data organizing skills, like Bryanna.

Bryanna's heart flitted as she neared the glass doors of Cognitivus. Tio, the entrance guard whose eyes reminded her of Kianto's, was on duty for the night.

"Happy seeing, Bryanna," Tio said, waving and smiling warmly as she walked in. "Hope the rains don't come to stay."

"Hope not, Tio," Bryanna replied, lingering around the elevators. "Looked like light clouds to me anyway." She knew she had to get started quickly, but Tio's eyes did that to her every time—made her slow down and dream.

If only Kianto had lived, Bryanna thought as the elevator zoomed up to the twelfth floor.

The floor, a sprawling, glass-windowed expanse peppered with workstations and portals for the technicians, was shrouded in darkness when Bryanna stepped off the elevator. No one was around, as expected. Data organizers like Bryanna came in only when the regular staff was gone and the day's work complete—it was more efficient that way. And the timing suited Bryanna perfectly, which she had discovered within a few months of starting at Cognitivus.

It was all because of that niggling doubt, that speck of sand she could not manage to shake out of her shoe.

What if Kianto fell prey to some wicked plot? What if the ODS had something to do with his death?

Bryanna had tried to shut it out but, like all doubts, this one was stubborn as well. What if she checked the ODS records just to make sure no one else had suffered a similar fate? A data organizer at Cognitivus could run a quick check. It was not going to harm anyone, only settle her concerns.

Bryanna had not expected to find nine sudden—largely unexplained as well—deaths at the ODS, all within a span of five years. Each of the unfortunate souls was in good, if not perfect, health. No one had been ailing, and each had been close to a high-ranking person at the ODS. Something sinister was afoot, Bryanna had been convinced. The niggling doubt had won, and Bryanna had plunged headfirst into a life of spying on the ODS.

Even though Bryanna did not uncover an obvious trend lurking in the ODS's records, the investigation gave her a sense of purpose, her life a new meaning. Like every other night in the past eight years, when she hurried into the Cognitivus that night, Bryanna forgot the pain in her hips and her wobbling gait. She only yearned to be at her terminal.

She needed to be alone, because she did more than she was supposed to do. On top of clearing and organizing each day's traffic through the information pipelines owned by Cognitivus, Bryanna also looked at other things. This was how she had found out—after two years of probing, no less—about the classified notes the ODS medic had made after inspecting Kianto's body. Notes that suggested the death was unusual. She had also discovered that the medic recommended a detailed autopsy, a suggestion the foundation turned down. It was odd that Sister Paramount Magetha refused Kianto's case the scrutiny it deserved, given that Kianto was her favored assistant at the time of his death and working on one of her pet projects.

Magetha!

Bryanna's fists clenched whenever she thought of the Sister Paramount. She knew, just like she knew that morning would follow the night, that Magetha had something to do with Kianto's death. Maybe because of Sister Magetha's refusal to pursue Kianto's case, or maybe it was a mother's intuition, but Magetha and her Order never felt right. But . . . it did not matter what she thought. Magetha was Sister Paramount at the ODS, way up in the heavens, way out of her reach. To get at her, Bryanna would need more than accusations and hunches; she'd need rock-hard proof.

Bryanna settled down at her portal and, within a few keystrokes, she was at the Organization Gallery. She coasted into the system, highlighting the current date. The screens flickered and subportals opened up, bringing her to what she was seeking. From here she could see the files recording every electronic transaction that had been made in this subdivision of Ajokkan, up until that moment. She could see how much a tourist had paid for an iced cone at Dobergon Plaza, all the arrests the constabularies had made during the day, every birth and death in the subdivision. There were close to a million transactions to be checked and retagged, Bryanna calculated.

Not too bad. She would have time to spare.

Her expert eyes flitted over the listings and focused on the transactions tagged with the Order of Divine Sight. Like always, she planned to start with them. With all records related to the ODS, Bryanna inspected deeper than she was expected to as a data organizer. She scrutinized more than an employee of the Cognitivus was allowed. Bryanna did not care or worry about the liberty she took. This was her way of keeping watch on Magetha and her organization. Maybe, Bryanna hoped, Magetha would slip again. Criminals always did. Only this time, Bryanna would be waiting.

Obviously, she could not tell anyone about her plan since that would mean disclosing her processes and highlighting the illegality of it. That would, at least, cost her the job and her only means to get to the bottom of her suspicions. Depending on what charges they brought against her, she could even face the firing squad. So, other than Nico, no one knew what she was up to.

Bryanna scanned the records—purchases, donations, a few new visions. Nothing out of the ordinary. She sighed. As much as she hoped to find that one loose end, there was never anything out of place in the foundation's operations. She tallied the number of transactions—404 in all—which matched the tally in the master sheet. She did not need to, but just like she did every day, Bryanna went into the logs and cross-checked every incoming storage request bearing the tag of the foundation.

Four hundred and five?

She sat up immediately, barely flinching at the piercing pain in her hips the sudden movement had brought on.

Why didn't the numbers match?

Bryanna counted the transactions one by one. There was still one transaction missing. A recording glitch? She shook her head and drove the thought away. Glitches did not happen at the Cognitivus.

Ten times she counted, back and forth. The irregularity remained.

For a moment, Bryanna thought of filing a report. Then she hesitated. She pored over the log, matching every transaction to its request, until she came to the stray.

The request—a stream of electronic pulses—had come in the early hours of the morning and done *something*. Only there was no testament of what it had done. It was like the stream of pulses had simply vanished without a trace.

As she cradled her throbbing head in palms that were rapidly turning cold and damp, Bryanna came to realize the impossible implication of her find: she was looking at an alteration command. Someone had sent a command to alter or delete a data record.

FEAR

Noell Rivans

The ruckus downstairs had almost died down and Noell's heavy lids had closed for just a bit when someone rapped on the door. She sat up on the bed like an uncoiled spring, her senses on alert. Instinctively, she pulled the threadbare shawl around her sleeping children, as if to hide them.

It took her a moment to get her bearings straight. She was not on Robben-Xiu 4217 anymore. She was in Ajokkan, at the Waterside Alehouse. They were safe for the moment, Noell reminded herself.

The rap, firm and impatient, sounded again.

Noell pulled her veil forward and took cautious steps toward the door. She closed her eyes on reaching it, mumbling a rushed prayer before she spoke.

"Who is it?" she managed a broken whisper.

"It's me, Noell," a man's voice replied.

Noell let out a long breath on recognizing the voice. Her frigid, stiff fingers fumbled at the locks for what seemed like forever until they fell open.

"Uncle Arum!" she exclaimed, smiling at the green-haired man, her father's older brother, hunched in the shabby corridor outside. "Come in." Noell opened the door wide.

Arum shot a quick look around before he stepped inside and closed the door behind him. Noell lit the oil lamp, twisting hard at its patina-covered wick raiser that had a habit of getting stuck. A flickering light, somewhat sad and dispiriting, spread to the corners of the tiny room.

"Come here, my dear," Arum called, pulling Noell into a tight embrace. His eyes were glistening when he let go. "Could barely speak to you when you arrived," he said. "Didn't want to draw too much attention."

"I understand," Noell replied. She had already drawn enough attention the moment she stepped into the alehouse. A woman, two children in tow, showing up after dark at a remote tavern had to raise some eyebrows. Capital of the Empire or not, even Ajokkan maintained some boundaries.

"I'm glad you came," Arum said. He took small, cautious steps around the room as if afraid of crashing into something. "Never imagined things would turn out this way when I saw you at your wedding."

Noell turned away and fixed her gaze on the darkness outside the window. She had not imagined this either. Yes, she was scared, but never in her worst nightmares had she thought of being on the run from her own husband. How long had it been? Yes, three days. They had been free for barely three days. It was too soon to rejoice, to unwind. Luca was a determined man and he was not one likely to let go of his possessions that easily.

"Noell," Uncle Arum asked gingerly, "your parents. Do they —"

"No. They don't know I left Luca." Noell knew she was being rude, cutting him off like that, but suddenly she did not care. She was not ready to talk about the parents who would not help their offspring when she was in mortal danger.

Arum stood with his head bowed, toe busily poking at the grimy floor. *Too embarrassed to ask,* Noell thought. Just like she was embarrassed to tell. How could she tell him how Luca had been beating her since the first month of their marriage? That he had been beating her at the most trivial of pretexts? One day it was her forgetting to water a plant, the next it was because she had knotted his shoelaces wrong. Luca spoke to her through his kicks, punches, and blows.

Lately, even Eos had not been escaping unscathed. She was only a baby when he had slapped her for crying too loud. Noell had thrown herself over the infant, shielding her from more blows. He had kicked her instead, but Noell bore the abuse happily. At least her child was safe. Since then, she took special care to keep Eos, and Jovan after her, out of Luca's sight. Sometimes she failed. Yet, she could not muster enough courage to leave. She had stayed with him for seven years, lingered with some unreasonable hope.

Other prickly issues arose, tall and strong, forming an unending maze around her and stopping her from leaving. There was no dodging them, no wishing them away. Like the fact that she had no way to support herself if she left, even if she escaped Luca's long reach, and the fact that her own parents would not take a stand against the monster in Noell's life.

Her mother had noticed the bruises on Noell's arms, Luca's wild temper, and even his blatant dallying with any woman he could lay his hands on. She had pretended to not see.

"He still keeps you, doesn't he?" her mother had countered when Noell told her. "Be grateful for that. We have good lives because of him. We all have to remember that. We owe him."

You owe me, Noell had thought. *I'm paying with my life for your comfort.* She had not said a thing to her mother though, only silently crumbled inside.

Remembering her mother's words did what it always did — left her feeling hollow and spent. Noell shuddered. She wanted to cry. No, she wanted to scream until she had no strength left in her.

"Noell." Arum's gentle voice nudged her senses.

Noell suppressed another shiver and fought the barrage of tears. *No more!* She had wept enough. She had endured enough. She did not owe anyone anything. She was not going to take the humiliation anymore. She deserved respect and she was going to fight until she got it. She could not let Eos grow up seeing her mother treated like an animal. And she could not let anyone treat Eos like she was any less than a princess.

A scarce bit of courage coursed through her veins, and Noell blurted, "I couldn't let him hurt Eos. I'm her mother. I had to protect her. I—" Tears flooded her eyes and a tight ache in her throat snuffed out her words.

Shuffling closer, Arum placed a hand on her head. Even while she struggled to restrain the unending tears that gushed out of her, Noell felt his hand tremble. *Is he afraid?*

"It'll be all right, child," Arum said. "I'll keep you safe. Hush now."

Noell wiped away her tears and held Arum's clammy hand in hers. "Uncle Arum, I came to you because you're the only family who I knew would give me shelter. But I don't want to be a weight on you. Find me some work."

"Weight?" Arum chuckled. "You'll be no weight. You're like a daughter to me, a daughter I never had. And no daughter can be a burden to her father, remember that." He paused to take a deep, long breath. "But I can't keep you with me, you understand?"

"I know, people would talk."

Arum chuckled again, longer this time. "I don't care what people say. Truth is I'm scared."

"Of what?" The words stung Noell's throat like the parched wastelands of Robben-Xiu.

Arum looked away at the darkened corner where the two children slept quietly.

"I need to send you as far away from me as I can." Arum's voice was dark. "That way . . . no one will know you're here."

"You also think . . ." Noell's voice faded. "You think he'll come after me?"

"Don't you?"

Pulling up every bit of strength she could scrounge from within her, Noell said the last thing she wanted to utter, lest it came true.

"I know he will."

As if from a world away, she heard the children stir. This had to end. She had to stop being afraid. If not for her sake, then for theirs.

"I'll be ready when he does."

Noell was done being afraid of her monster of a husband.

FACE

Mako Nuyin

It was past midnight when Mako reached his home, a two-story row house on the posh Avenue of Marcessa. Seeing the dark windows, he breathed a sigh of relief. Orin, his father, was sleeping, thank the heavens for that.

After Mako's mother passed away a year ago, his father had moved in with him. Mako had hoped it would turn out well; at least it'd be easier for him to care for the man who was rapidly losing his eyesight, but things had turned rather explosive.

Orin was not happy with anything Mako had chosen — profession, lifestyle, values — and he did not think twice about making his low opinions of his son known. It wasn't always like this. Mako found it hard to believe that he had been closer to his father when he was younger. Something snapped when Mako chose to work for the Intelligence Bureau. His father simply shut Mako out, labeled him a failure, and almost overnight he'd turned into a vitriol-spewing, bitter old man. All because Mako had refused to become an Imperial soldier like his father.

Mako punched the keys to the front door and pushed it open as noiselessly as he could. An ache had invaded his head, and Mako was not in the mood to put up with his father's usual lectures about being late. Tiptoeing, he crossed the hallway and had barely stepped into the grand room when a bright beam of light fell on his face, blinding him.

"Father!" Mako yelled, shading his eyes.

"Look who finally found his way home," Orin jeered, his flashlight steady on Mako as he stumbled toward the wall.

Mako groaned as he felt for the light controls. "This is why I don't come home. Because you hound me like I'm a fugitive."

The shelf. And there, the controls. A soft light flooded the room as his hand twisted the lacquered knob.

"If you don't want me to hound you, maybe you could get home at a decent hour," his father retorted.

"Father!" Mako blinked to let his eyes adjust to the light. "I'm not a little boy anymore. Can you please remember that?"

"I will. When you get your life in order," his father said, grunting as he got off his armchair.

"My life's fine, Father. I'm doing well. I've got a great career, I—"

Orin scoffed. "You call spying a career? There's no honor in spying, none at all. Go ask anyone."

Mako stared at his father. Bald, rotund, and slightly hunched, there was no remaining sign that once upon a time this man had been a dashing, honorable soldier in the Forces.

"I make good money," Mako said. He made in a month what soldiers like his father made in years.

"For what?" his father asked. His eyes were wide, neck muscles bulging. "What do you need money for when you don't have a life?"

As much as Mako wanted to calm down, his father's remarks kept that anger frothing inside.

Orin shuffled closer and patted his shoulder. "You need to find a wife, Mako. Settle down. It's time."

Mako edged away. "I do *not* need a wife," he declared crossly. "I'm fine this way."

His father did not understand that Mako cherished his freedom. A wife would slow him down; cut his wings off, so to speak. Close to being the top agent in the Imperial Intelligence Bureau, Mako did not need distractions or anchors.

"I'm going to get some sleep, Father," he said in the firmest tone he could manage. "You should too. It's late."

Orin threw his arms up and rolled his eyes. "Whatever are we going to do with the boy?"

"What boy?"

"The one I have had stashed in the cellar since morning," Orin replied with a casual wave.

Mako froze. He could not breathe, let alone speak.

The rage that had been churning inside him relentlessly vanished and only a whisper escaped his suddenly parched lips. "Stashed? What in the Niappan's name have you done?"

***

The boy was a huddled heap in the corner of the damp cellar. His face had a sickly yellow tinge. Gray hair, matted and grungy, hung over his forehead in an unruly mess. He was young, about thirteen or fourteen years old. His eyes—the irises faded to almost white—were the weirdest Mako had ever seen. Those, along with his skeletal frame, gave the boy an almost macabre look. He sprung forward on seeing Mako, flashing a quick, toothy smile.

"Roli?" Mako exclaimed. "What are you doing here?" Even as he asked that question, Mako knew. What Arum had told him was perhaps truer than he had hoped it would be. The boy had definitely seen a murder, and possibly of an oracle.

"I need to talk to you about something," Roli replied. He pointed an unsteady finger at Orin, who had followed Mako down to the cellar. "First, he has to leave."

Orin scoffed and rolled his eyes. "I let you into the house because you said you knew Mako. I fed you. I hid you just like you wanted. I didn't press for an explanation because you said you'd tell when Mako got here. And now you want me to leave without hearing why? Aren't you an ungrateful—" Orin would have continued spiritedly, but Mako stopped him.

"Father, please. You can see he's nervous. Let's not scare him more," Mako whispered in his father's ear. Sliding an arm over Orin's shoulder, Mako turned him around and led him to the stairs. "Get some sleep. I'll talk to you in the morning."

Mako turned to face Roli when his father's form disappeared from view. The boy stood with his arms crossed, his pale eyes darting around the room incessantly.

"Your father's good, but a little nutty," he declared.

Mako chuckled. Hastily wiping the dust off a small table in the corner, he beckoned Roli.

"Tell me, Roli. Why are you here?"

The boy slumped on the chair Mako pulled out for him. "He said your name . . . I think," Roli blurted, trembling a little.

"Who?"

"Your friend, the oracle."

Mako held his arms up. "Wait. My friend?"

"I've seen you with him at the alehouse," Roli insisted. "He has long yellow hair, brown eyes. He usually wears a white tunic with gold stars."

"Leon?" Mako muttered, suddenly craving a glass of cool, spiced water. He slumped into a chair and leaned against the table, thankful for its sturdy presence. The white tunic and gold stars implied an oracle prime, and the only one Mako knew and met at the alehouse was Leon.

Leon Courtee, Oracle Prime at the Order of Divine Sight, was a family friend. Mako had known him since he was a boy. Back in the old neighborhood near the northern city limits where Mako grew up, Leon's house stood next to theirs. Leon was the friendly neighbor next door, the kind everyone wishes for but few are lucky enough to have. Leon was Mako's hero not only because he had the gift of divination, but because he was a true friend. While Mako's father was away at the front and proudly serving the Empire as a loyal soldier, Leon was often the one who fixed Mako's swing or mended his toy.

All these years, they had kept in touch. Once in a while, Leon met Mako at the alehouse, seeking help with minor cases — a petty theft here, a dispute there — that Mako took up on the side.

Is . . . is Leon dead?

"I remembered his face and he kept saying your name, so . . ." Roli rocked back and forth in a gentle rhythm.

"Roli!" Mako called sharply, grabbing the boy's shoulder. "What did you see *exactly?*"

"The metal man," Roli said, his lips trembling. "He . . . he . . . sliced up your friend."

"Wha—" Mako's question remained unasked. A metal man? That sounded like something out of a storybook. The fear in Roli's wide eyes seemed real though. But was it possible? Someone had murdered an oracle in broad daylight and no one even knew?

"So, I'm camped in a house in the tannery rows," Roli said. "Suddenly, I hear some strange noises outside and . . . I see your friend lying on the road, bleeding all over and . . . this man with metal arms and legs is stabbing him . . ." Roli's voice cracked as a violent shiver broke over him. "I crawl downstairs and I peep through the windows and . . ."

Roli pulled his knees to his chest, wrapped his arms around them, and started rocking again.

"What happened then?"

"I'm peeping through the shutter downstairs when I catch your friend's . . . Leon's . . . eyes."

"And?"

"He sort of . . . tells me things. I hear his voice in my head."

Mako stiffened. "He told you things? How? He screamed while the metal man was . . . murdering him?"

"No, I heard it in my head. He was *in* my head."

This was getting more unbelievable by the moment. Leon was in his head? Had Roli been using smokepots? It was possible. No, make that likely. Who knew what a vagrant like Roli was up to?

Mako's incredulity must have shown in his face, because Roli frowned and his cheeks took on a bright flush.

"You think I'm lying?" he snapped. "He's an oracle. He can do things. He must've sent a brain wave or something."

Mako composed himself. The throbbing in his head was only growing stronger. This needed to be wrapped up quickly.

"All right," he said, patting Roli reassuringly. "What did he tell you?"

Roli looked away, his lips puckered in an indignant pout.

"Roli." Mako leaned forward to catch his gaze. "I'm sorry. It's just that I haven't heard anything like this before. What you're describing almost sounds like telepathy but—"

"But what?" Roli snapped.

"Oracles use telepathy, sure," Mako started explaining. "But people like you and I can't. So even if my friend knew telepathy, he would have a hard time speaking to you through brain waves."

Unless . . .

Thoughts tumbled in his mind. He had read about something once, in one of those books on ancient unsolved mysteries. They called it "transference," the ability to push thoughts telepathically to people, even nonpracticing people. But . . . those books were no scientific treatise, simply a collection of half-truths built on ancient myths.

"You think I've been smoking or something?" Roli glared. "Well, I don't smoke. And I haven't heard anything like this either, but I know what happened to me." The boy paused to draw a sharp breath or two. "You think I'm liking this? I've been hiding all day. Haven't worked, haven't slept, and wouldn't have had a bite to eat if your father didn't give me some food."

"I'm sorry, Roli. Really am."

Roli looked away moodily for a while. "When your friend looked at me, I felt strange," he said finally. "Like I could hear him. Like he was whispering in my ear."

Could it really be transference on a commoner? Oracles often practiced ancient forgotten arts. Perhaps Leon had rediscovered the art of transference? But transferring to an ordinary citizen, particularly a squatter like Roli? There had to be real urgency. Had Leon . . . Mako stopped the notion right there. It could not be Leon . . . had to be some other oracle.

"What did he tell you?"

"He asked me to find Mako Nuyin at the Waterside Alehouse. That's you, right?"

Mako nodded. The oracle was indeed looking for him. And who else but Leon would know to find him at that alehouse? Not every oracle could know transference either. It had to be Leon.

Roli continued in a faint voice, "I had to tell you that the prophecy is a lie. They erased his vision. The real Adi Niappan is a girl, he said. Her name is Eos and she has a mark on her forehead. Wait . . . he said the mark of the moon."

Mako blinked a few times to fully grasp the meaning of Roli's words. The boy was talking about the Eternity Prophecy. But . . . how could the Eternity Prophecy be a lie? Leon's own cluster had announced the new Adi Niappan's identity. Could the head of ODS have lied at the Conclave?

Mako shook his head vehemently to drive the thought away. Now he was sure he was going crazy.

But what else could Leon have meant? And how did this girl fit in?

Strands of thought began to stray and fade as he puzzled and Mako realized he was too tired. His brain could not think clearly anymore.

"What happened to the body?" he asked, rising to his feet.

"The metal man blew him up."

"Blew him *up*?" Mako could not stop his voice from rising.

Not only did this metal man kill an oracle, but he blew up the body in broad daylight? This was some tale Roli was spinning.

"Yes, his body just . . . went *pop*!"

"Pop? As in, fell to pieces?"

Roli nodded vigorously. "Yes. But not pieces. Tiny balls. Red balls. A gazillion of them."

Mako did not know what to say, so he simply held his breath.

"Then the metal man's helper sucked the balls into a canister. Sprinkled some powdery white stuff on the ground."

"There's a helper too?"

Roli nodded and flailed his arms above his head. "He has real big, fluffy yellow hair. He was wearing a brown . . . overall . . . tunic, sort of. Actually, they both were."

No matter how impossible everything sounded, Mako knew he had to look into the matter. Problem was, he only had a day before he left on his mission to Robben-Xiu. There was so much to be done for the mission and little time for this. Still, he had to do something.

He decided to visit the Order of Divine Sight in the morning to make sure Leon was all right.

KILL

Steffen Pere

The whisper was like an icy breeze ripping through a warm autumn afternoon, leaving a rustle of leaves in its wake. It blew Fia's soft curls just a little to let the sun shine on her laughing eyes.

"Master Pere." The whisper was light, yet insistent. "You have an Imperial summons."

Fia's little feet kicked the heaps and the fallen leaves — red, orange, yellow — took to the wind in a rush of color. She laughed; the tinkle spread like a cascade through the air and flooded Steffen's heart.

"Master?"

The afternoon ripped around the edges. Steffen tried to hold on to Fia, but she receded, her rosy face crumbling into specks of dust.

No! Wait!

"Master, there's a summons waiting."

The afternoon collapsed on itself and melted into pitch black.

Steffen opened his eyes; his mechanical one came into sharp focus in an instant while the one made of flesh and blood struggled through the haze of his broken dream.

A young man with fluffy golden hair stood cowering in front of Steffen's recharging station, his gaze skimming the floor, his eyes dark and jittery. A slight touch on the inlaid switch parted the glass doors of the enclosure and let the cool air escape. Steffen shifted slightly, seeking a comfortable position for his spine. His recharging station — a necessity for a man with innumerable electromechanical implants that needed regular power boosts — was state of the art, but spending a long time in what was essentially an upright glass casket was not an enjoyable exercise. And now that his routine had been interrupted, he would need to spend even longer in the contraption.

"Yes, Tors?" Steffen said through grinding teeth, smiling a little as he noticed the man shudder. His assistant deserved to be jumpy, ruining a dream of Fia like that.

Tors shifted on his feet. "The Imperial summons again, Master."

Steffen took a deep breath. Anger did not come to him so quick, but it was brewing for sure. He was not used to summonses anymore; those days of being at the beck and call of the Empire was something he hoped to have left behind. Heading the Imperial Assassin Corps was all he thought about now. He had been promised the position and he deserved it after his long, honorable service to the Empire as Master Assassin. He did not like these summonses; however, as much as he disliked it, an Imperial summon was not something he could ignore.

"Patch it in," he instructed.

As Tors hurried away, Steffen closed his eyes and waited for the visual. Like always, his assistant Tors was quick to direct the communication to the receiver embedded in Steffen's brain. It came in like a wave, sprawling across Steffen's consciousness in the form of an ornate scroll stamped with the Imperial insignia. The sound — the steely voice of a machine — came right after the insignia dissolved away.

"Is the task complete?" the voice asked.

"Yes."

"Witnesses?"

His lips thinned. Master Assassin Steffen Pere, however long his retirement from active duty as an Imperial assassin might have been, knew how to avoid having witnesses. He would not be vetted as head of the Imperial Assassin Corps if he were in the habit of leaving loose ends.

"None," he replied.

"Payment has been sent."

"Thank you."

"Prepare for next assignment."

Steffen held his breath. There wasn't supposed to be a next. This was supposed to have been his last assignment before he took the official vows as the head of Assassin Corps.

"Id 426-YS-83080."

"Timeline?" Steffen's voice trembled.

Is it excitement? he wondered, cringing a little at the thought. *They are sucking me in once again.*

"Study the subject," the steely, lifeless voice instructed. "Hold for elimination order."

The communication ended with a sharp click.

Thoughts, questions mostly, swarmed Steffen like a pack of unrelenting bees. There was not supposed to be another assignment, yet here he was, waiting.

And why can't I finish the new target off right away? Why did they ask me to hold?

Perhaps the would-be target wasn't a threat yet? That meant there was a chance they'd never be a threat, and the assassination order would be called off.

Something that felt a lot like disappointment twitched inside Steffen at the thought.

Aren't I supposed to be happy if the order is called off? Isn't that what I've hoped for – to be done with the killing?

The questions stilled. Steffen sat for a while, his mind blank and his limbs prone. Then, with swift deliberation, he got off the recharging station and walked toward the courtyard where Tors was busy cooking their meal.

"Tors!" he called, flexing his metallic fingers in a slow, rhythmic motion.

Killing that oracle had stirred the feelings he had suppressed for so long. It made him yearn again for the sensations – the smell of freshly spilled blood, soft flesh ripping at the touch of his knife, the rush from seeing life ebb away as he stared into terrified eyes.

"Master Pere." Tors hurried forward, head bowed, gaze stuck

firmly on the ground.

"Is the pit empty?"

Tors looked up at him as if a whip had struck him. His face twisted before his lips quivered with a nervous smile. He nodded slowly, as if hesitating to break the news.

That was expected. A couple of years ago, before Steffen had resigned from Imperial service, the pit would always be full. Back then, his thirst for fresh kill was insatiable. Every day he needed a prey to feast on, so on days there was no official assignment, Steffen turned to the pit.

The pit, an underground holding cell, held hapless prey — stray animals, sometimes even a vagrant human or two — to satisfy his need to kill. Killing was the only way he could fulfill his urges and maintain his sanity.

That need was back again.

"Get something for the night," he instructed Tors.

It was time to kill some more.

2

Respect madness and disorder, for it is the cradle of a superior future, it is where new order is born.

—Adi Niappan of the long eclipse

CONFERRAL

The Adi Niappan's palace rested like a bloodied crown on top of Ajokkan's only high ground, the Mal Yorah. Built with rare red-and-yellow starstone that caught the rays of the system's two suns long before the rest of Ajokkan, the palace was, just like its famous denizen, a world apart from the rest of the Empire.

All through the week following the announcement of the Eternity Prophecy, the normally quiet outer courtyard of the palace had been abuzz. Now, at this latest event, the Imperial Council — proxy leaders of the Empire while the Adi Niappan was incapacitated — had assembled the heads of Ajokkan's leading oracle clusters. Large round tables covered with scarlet cloth dotted the yard. The table nearest to the palace stairs and the provisional high podium at its foot was reserved for the chief dignitaries. The star among them was Sister Paramount Magetha, head of the Order of Divine Sight, the oracle cluster that had produced the most recent Eternity Prophecy.

As soon as the appreciation address by Ravea Phiser, Principal of the Imperial Council, came to an end, people flocked to Magetha to show their respect. She deserved much more than an appreciation address, they whispered, for she had saved them and the Empire. So they surrounded her, bowing, kneeling, stooping, until the entire assembly had bowed, kneeled, and stooped time and again.

A sumptuous meal, ten courses served in exquisite crystal salvers, followed. It was not until two hours later that Sister Paramount Magetha rose to leave. Her entourage of five low-level oracles rushed to her side immediately.

Principal Ravea Phiser approached as Magetha's assistants bustled and fussed around her. "Allow me the honor of seeing you to your transport."

Magetha smiled and, waving her entourage away, walked to the principal's side. Thiers was a powerful and purposeful walk, strides matching each other's in perfect synchrony. About ten paces behind them, the hushed entourage followed.

"The Empire cannot thank you enough for the vision you have bestowed on us," Ravea said as they walked across the terrace. "We will be whole again."

"It was my honor," Magetha replied, her voice guttural and stiff. "It was not an easy task. There are a few ripples still."

"You know you have my support. Our support. The entire . . . almost the entire council is with you."

"Almost?" Magetha's voice rose a little.

"There is always a dissenter when you need them the least."

"Do I not know that already?"

"Look past the distractions. We . . . *you* have found a way to keep the Empire whole by bringing New Haphniss into the fold. That is a progress we should celebrate. The Empire will be forever thankful for our efforts."

"We have not brought New Haphniss into the fold yet."

"But we will. It is only a matter of time now. The rebel vermin on New Haphniss know this as well as we do—Imperial decrees can be ignored under false pretenses, but not the Eternity Prophecy. They have to either accept the Adi Niappan's tenets or refute them openly. If they yield to us, their allegiance will be an example for rest of the Empire. If they challenge, we shall crush them and the rest of the Empire will learn to obey. Either way, we shall win."

Magetha nodded hastily, like a nervous bird pecking at seeds as fast as it could. "If only we can quell the dissent," she muttered.

"We shall. I have faith in Master Pere. You should as well."

Their steps slowed on nearing the bloodred state transport that awaited Magetha.

"My foundation would like to help in New Haphniss."

"Certainly. Yours will be the one and only cluster on New Haphniss when we bring the colony in. Just like we agreed." Ravea parted the door screen for Sister Paramount Magetha. "Pleasant seeing."

"Pleasant seeing, Principal Phiser," she replied before climbing into the dark insides of the state transport.

QUESTION

Mako Nuyin

The Order of Divine Sight was like the rest of the oracle clusters in the Empire—its premises were heavily guarded with high stone walls topped with barbed wire. Usually the sprawling compounds had only a few entrances, all monitored by live guards as well as sophisticated motion-capture systems. Mako Nuyin reached the foundation's main doorway early in the morning. He was screened twice and patted down a few times before he was allowed inside the public relations building.

Thoughts crowded Mako's head in a tempestuous churn as he followed the escort guard inside.

What had Leon—no, not Leon! It could be someone else. Someone else who looked like Leon and perhaps had heard about Mako. Yes, that had to be it. Now, what did the murdered oracle mean about the Eternity Prophecy being false? Had Roli misunderstood? Had a dying man muttered something bizarre in his final moments?

Or had Sister Paramount Magetha faked the Eternity prophecy—

No!

No one dared faking a prophecy, not even mundane ones related to matters as trivial as weather predictions, let alone the Eternity Prophecy.

But if they had, then was this girl really what the murdered oracle thought she was? Was she the real successor to the Adi Niappan?

No! Mako sneered at the idea. It was too fantastic a claim to be true. *A girl as an Adi Niappan would be absurd.*

Mako looked around, desperate to find something to distract his wayward ideas. Thankfully, he was not left alone for too long. A white-bearded man who introduced himself as Jacen, the Principal of Meetings, saw him in a room with dark-lacquered walls where the escort guard had left Mako waiting.

"Pleasant seeing," said Jacen, smiling. He bowed just a little at Mako. "May I be of assistance?"

"I'm here to meet Oracle Prime Courtee," Mako blurted the practiced lines, studying Jacen as he spoke. Mako worried that it came off sounding too rehearsed. "Leon's expecting me," he added a lie.

Jacen tried to give Mako a bigger smile. His mouth was stretched to its limit, so now his cheeks swelled some more and his eyes crinkled. Mako found his cheerfulness a bit odd. People at these foundations were nothing if not arrogant. The officials at the oracle clusters were an entitled bunch. They were the herders of the all-seeing oracles, whose visions drove the mighty Veloressian Empire forward. They had reason to be haughty.

The likes of Mako coming to meet one of their oracles should not have been an occasion to smile. Typically, Mako would have been given the proverbial cold shoulder, a brush-off. The oracle would be reprimanded later for inviting a commoner to the foundation premises. Yet, Jacen, the Principal of Meetings, had not only come to greet Mako in person, but also seemed remarkably happy about it.

"Ah, yes." Jacen nodded with such familiarity as if a hundred people had come to visit Leon Courtee today. "Oracle Prime Courtee, of course. Let me see . . ."

Jacen slid into one of the high-backed chairs lined up along the walls and closed his eyes.

Mako barely stopped his head from shaking. *The foundation and its pretentious ways,* he scoffed under his breath. Jacen could've simply used a portal but instead used his mentanet.

Mentanets were telepathic communication networks used by the oracles and lesser prescients at the foundations. Instead of the regular information channels that used electronic streams to transfer data, mentanets used thoughts. A foundation's most private network was telepathic, made up of connected thought streams. Almost every oracle cluster had its own mentanet with specific transfer and flow protocols that no outsider could breach. Other than being a source of awe for the regular Veloressians, the mentanets were also secure and provided extreme privacy. To Mako, the principal's using a mentanet at the moment seemed like overkill.

As if awakened from deep slumber, Jacen opened his startled green eyes. He smiled again, although this time it took him more effort than before.

"A moment, please." Holding up a finger, Jacen rushed to one corner of the room, where an antique writing desk stood camouflaged among the walls, and picked up a missive pad. He strode hurriedly over to Mako and handed him the pad and a pen. "The fuss with the Eternity Prophecy has everyone in the Order enormously engaged. Oracle Prime Courtee is busier than everyone else since his duties are weightier than the rest."

Restless eyes, Mako noted. *The man is spinning a tale.*

"Can Leon see me?" Mako asked bluntly.

"I'm afraid not," Jacen replied, pursing his lips and shaking his head. "You could leave him a note. I'll pass it on to him right away. Although, knowing the work that will go on until the Eternity Prophecy is fulfilled, I doubt he'll find time for anything other than prophecy-related business."

In other words, Leon would be unreachable for a long time. Roli could've been right after all.

No, Mako thought, *I'm reading too much into this. Jacen makes perfect sense.*

The Eternity Prophecy was no easy business, especially when New Haphniss and the imminent war with the colony was in the mix. Leon could . . . would have his hands full.

"Leave a note?" Jacen's eager voice interrupted Mako's thoughts.

"Yes," Mako said. He was going to leave a message. It had to be succinct yet meaningful, and only something Leon himself could answer. After thinking for a moment, Mako started to write.

Father wants to pledge life to a foundation. Seeks conversion guidance.
~Mako

Leon would understand. Orin Nuyin—Mako's father and Leon Courtee's old chum—was not a spiritual man. Never had been. The elder Nuyin was the farthest away from the notion of Gods. Orin wanting to pledge himself to a foundation was just as absurd as a feline begging to take a bath. Leon, if he received that note, would surely contact Mako. If he did not, then Mako would be certain that Leon Courtee was no more.

REASON

Bryanna Tu-Fei

The tub, filled to the brim with near-scalding water infused with Lau-jasmine petals, engulfed Bryanna into folds of warm ecstasy. This was her guilty pleasure and a rare indulgence — the soak.

Before she was a data organizer at the Cognitivus, Bryana was a practical, frugal, and no-nonsense employee of the Imperial Education Services. Back then, she believed a soak was a waste like no other. Kianto loved them though, and Bryanna let him have one as a prize once in a while. For her, it was strictly a timed shower. A shower that was economical and also good for the natural balance. Then, after Kianto passed, Bryanna discovered the joys of a soak in a rather ironic turn of events.

She had filled the tub as another one of her experiments to invite death. Not knowing how to swim, drowning in that oversize tub would be easy, she had thought. After intoxicating herself with the strongest Roydonberry nectar, she had lowered herself into the tub. A few minutes later, she realized she was enjoying the arrangement . . . far too much to die of it. Then, after Nico arrived and Bryanna embraced life once again, she used a soak regularly, to relax and to rejuvenate herself.

Lying back on the curved incline of the tub, Bryanna looked around to account for everything she needed. Her state-of-the-art computing portal was hooked up close, at a safe distance from the water but near enough to recognize her voice commands. Next to her, on a niche crowded with knickknacks, a goblet sparkled with fresh Roydonberry nectar.

"Ahhh . . ." Bryanna let out a long sigh and closed her eyes. She was ready to roll. She had fed Nico and his brothers and sisters, so there was all the time in the world. Although, she had the highest confidence in her cats. They knew that when the tub was filled it was their cue to stay away and give Bryanna her space. Sensible creatures they were — the reason Bryanna respected them so.

Time to get some work done.

"Veloressia Felis." Bryanna used the portal's code name to command it to wakefulness. "Compare tally." Immediately, a silvery-blue orb rotated to life on the computing screen. Two screens opened side by side, highlighting the discrepancy Bryanna had uncovered the previous night. She had checked and rechecked the numbers many times, but the result was clear — an alteration command had indeed been sent.

By the Imperial Laws of Data Integrity, deletion of public records or modifying them was a crime punishable by a life term in prison. Everybody knew that, yet someone had had the guts to tamper with a public record. Why? Bryanna did not know, of course. Not yet.

"But I will," she whispered under her breath as she stared intently at the screen. Last night, after discovering the inconsistency, Bryanna had thought of filing a report. In the end, she had done nothing of the sort. Instead, Bryanna did the unthinkable.

She stole data.

Bryanna's spare data storage was the size of a thumbnail and she always carried it on her, just in case. She had never used it at the Cognitivus, never had the reason to. Seeing the divergence of data, knowing how closed the oracle clusters were to scrutiny and how deep their connections went, Bryanna realized the futility of filing a report at the Cognitivus. Just like Kianto's death had been hushed up, this irregularity would be written off, she was sure, as a failure of the communication channel.

Only Bryanna knew this was no random failure. This had to be intentional damage. The Order of Divine Sight was up to something, and she *had* to find out what it was. So Bryanna decided to commit a crime and steal the month's history of transactions from the ODS.

"All for a good cause," Bryanna murmured. "The truth above

everything."

She reached for the goblet of nectar and took a long sip, enjoying the warmth cascading down her throat.

"Order and match transactions and records," she said, then indulged in another sip. The orb spun for a bit and then the portal spewed out hundreds of entries in a neat line, sorted by their time of creation. Bryanna smiled, enjoying the efficiency of the program she had created to sort through piles of data. Kianto would have been so proud. Unfortunately, she had never shown any interest in the computing technologies when her son was alive, always thinking of herself as a staid kind of person with no knack for the flashy ways of the younger generation.

Beep! The transactions and records lined up perfectly, except for the twentieth record — one she now knew was an alteration command and had named AC 20 — sent in the wee hours of the morning. What more could she do with this? Taking a deep breath, Bryanna sank into the water until it came up to her chin.

"Let's see where you were sent," Bryanna muttered. Turning to the portal, she said, "Match destination coordinates with universal address list."

The spinning orb filled the screen — the portal was crosschecking the coordinates with a list of addresses that included the common destination of transactions.

Bryanna had time for two long sips before the orb came to a stop and faded away. A name flashed, and Bryanna blinked.

"Prophecy Archives?" Bryanna's disbelieving whisper floated up through the incense-laden air of the bath chamber.

It was a crime weighty enough to tamper with any public record. But to damage a record in the Prophecy Archives? That was as outrageous and as incredible as New Haphniss's claim that the Adi Niappan was not appointed by the Gods themselves.

Yet, it had been done. But who could have dared to do such a thing? And what record did they alter in the archives? Could someone have altered a prophecy?

No! No, no, no! Bryanna shoved the blasphemous thought out of her mind. The archives held other information, albeit related to prophecies, also. They stored histories, catalogs of unfinished visions, prophecy-related monetary transaction reports of the clusters, among many things. It had to be one of those incidental records.

"Let's find out which record you messed with," Bryanna muttered.

If she had access to all the data in the Prophecy Archives, it would be very easy to find what had been tampered with, but she did not have that luxury. However, she had collected — stolen, to be exact — all the records generated in the previous month from the ODS. That roughly translated to billions of records, but she could easily parse them. The alteration command that went into the Prophecy Archives had a field in it to identify the record it was sent to change and Bryanna had already extracted that. Now if only she could find a record matching that ID among all the data she had stolen . . .

"Start Rummager Version 4.0. Scan for record with ID in AC 20."

The silver orb started spinning again, and Bryanna sunk back into the warm folds of scented water. She still could not believe what was happening, that someone could have tampered with a public record, and a record at the Prophecy Archives at that. She had taken only five sips at the nectar when the portal beeped.

That was quick! Bryanna relished the surge of pride at her program's speed as she squinted at the screen. Splayed on it was a data record that looked similar to every other data record that passed through the Empire's extensive electronic networks every moment. It looked ordinary, except Bryanna knew it was not. It had to have contained something that someone in the ODS needed to change.

"You poor thing," Bryanna said, her heart twinging as she stared at the chunky record hovering on the screen. "What a wronged little entry you are."

Bryanna mused for a while, but she knew she could not do much with the record itself. Data records — particularly when travelling through the networks — were encrypted, and unscrambling one was next to impossible, even for her.

But if she could not decipher what was changed by opening up a record, then she had to find another way to understand what crime had been committed against it. The question was: how? Pursing her lips, Bryanna started thinking of her next step. She decided quickly — she'd start by finding who sent the unlawful alteration command.

"Bring up AC 20. Analyze origin coordinates," Bryanna said curtly, and the portal obliged almost in an instant, showing the coded origin coordinates for the irregular record.

Bryanna sat up, her hand reaching for the goblet stalling in midair. She recognized that coordinate well. It was a source from within the sisterhood's offices.

It did not make any sense. Sister Paramount Magetha, leader of the Order of Divine Sight, was a shrewd woman. She would not be rash enough to alter a record in the Prophecy Archives from her own premises. Or was she desperate enough to make such a misstep? Perhaps her arrogance made her think she was invincible. Or maybe, Magetha was not involved at all. Could one of Magetha's minions have done it without her knowing? Even though it would not be the outcome Bryanna's heart desired, it was possible. Either way, she had to find out. All Bryanna could see now was the point of origin. She needed to dig further down, pinpoint it to know who sent it, but there was no way to . . .

"Wait, wait, wait," Bryanna gushed. She knew how she could solve this, only voice commands would not help; she'd have to work with keystrokes.

The soak?

Hell, the soak could wait. Bryanna pulled herself up, careful not to stress her aching back. Dripping all over the mats, she wrapped a plush Lau-jasmine-scented robe around her. Then, scooping up the portal, Bryanna rushed out of the bath chamber.

Outside, Nico welcomed her with a loud yowl.

"I know, Nico," Bryanna mumbled, eyes blazing as she stared into her portal. "That was too quick, wasn't it? Well, I couldn't finish my soak. Have to get back in there again. But first, dear boy, your mother needs to sort this out."

WATCH

Steffen Pere

Steffen busily rubbed his elbow as he walked past the large glass-covered building of the Cognitivus. The mechanical joint at his elbow was too tightly strung. Any other time Steffen would be cursing, but at the moment, he was happy for the distraction. The exercise kept him from accidentally glancing at the glass panes next to him.

Years of practice went into avoiding a glimpse of his battered face. A decade had passed since his transformation, and yet Steffen could not bear looking at the horrid piece of flesh that was his face. Some days Steffen wished he had not survived the incursion that left him scarred. The medics had resurrected him, but his body was tattered. They fit a metal dome over his cleaved skull so his brains would not fall out. They stitched his face, put metal implants to even out the deepest gouges. His left eye was smashed, so a biomechanical one took its place. An arm and a leg were replaced also. He was an abomination—Steffen knew it all too well. He did not need the glass panes reminding him of it.

With considerable effort, fighting the thick fabric of his deep-brown overalls that were in the way of his probing fingers, Steffen detected the clamp he needed to adjust. Feeling for the flared ends, he gave the knob a practiced twist and it eased.

Just right, Steffen thought, flexing his arms a little. A cybernetic body like his came with its share of problems, like an accidental overtightening of a limb.

"Master," Tors whispered urgently as they walked side by side. "This place is crowded."

Steffen grunted in reply. He did not like to talk during assignments, but Tors never stopped. Once in a while, Steffen would shoot a glare at the young man, but that could only quiet him for an hour or two at most. Tors often appeared fearful, but Steffen knew he was quite tough inside.

"No chance of making it work during the day," Tors said in a bubbly voice.

Too much excitement, Steffen thought.

The new assignments were fun for Tors, even though they annoyed Steffen to no end. First, he did not like these trivial killings of pathetic people, like the oracle of the other day. He liked worthy adversaries, people who gave a stiff fight. Conquering a smart and swift prey . . . now that was a hunt worth remembering.

"She works on a night shift at Cognitivus though," Tors said, his brown eyes shining even in the shadow his oversized cowl cast on them. "Maybe we can meet her on her way in."

"No, has to be on her way out."

"Way out?" Tors squawked. "But that'll be in the morning. People will see."

"Can't let people see."

"But the night's easier. It's dark and —"

"Has to be the morning," Steffen snarled through gritted teeth. So many years with him, and Tors still understood so little. If they attacked the woman before her shift, the Cognitivus would miss their data organizer immediately. They could start looking. If they got her in the morning, no one except those damned cats would miss her. There'd be a whole day to tie up any loose ends.

Tors blinked rapidly a few times. "All right," he said after a while. "Guess we have to find a good spot to get to her. Maybe we get inside her house?"

"Hmm . . ." Steffen replied. He hated to think of the next target assigned to him. A dumpy old woman with a bunch of cats? He had a cold and calm brain, but this thought set his head on fire every time. First, he, Master Assassin Pere, the vetted head of the Imperial Assassin Corps, had been ordered out of retirement into killing an overweight oracle. And now this? Even Tors could get this job done.

"Master?" Tors piped up. "The same place across the street?"

"Yes," Steffen replied. "Get a table away from the door this time."

They were headed to Tuntun's, a tiny little café. On one side of it was a behemoth bookstore that spread the aroma of crusty books all over the sidewalk. Its other neighbor was a shop with a sickly green-and-pink facade full of useless antiques and knickknacks. In between them stood the café—Tuntun's—with food that was tolerable, drinks that were bordering on atrocious, and an ambience that was hardly inviting. It was as if someone had decided to haul some chairs and tables in, set up a stove in one corner, put up a sign over the doorway, and started selling food. It was surprising that people came in at all. Yet, they did. Steffen ran a finger across one of the café tables on the sidewalk, his mouth curling in disgust as the act left a shiny trail through a layer of grime. Steffen drew in a long breath to calm his flaring temper. Unfortunate as it was, Tuntun's was the only way; its location was perfect for keeping an eye on the target's house.

Turning away, he waited for his assistant to get back. Tors arrived soon, huffing in excitement. His hood had slipped off his head and his fluffy golden hair stood like a bushy floret. "Master," he said, not understanding the furious glare Steffen shot at him. "Mara's got the perfect table for us. Come this way."

"Cover your face," Steffen hissed. "Who's Mara?"

"The girl who served us yesterday." Tors seemed tediously giddy talking about the girl.

"The one with the purple eyes?"

Steffen remembered the girl with purple eyes very clearly. He also remembered light brown hair, a pear-shaped face, a figure that curved and swelled a little too much in places, and a dress that highlighted each of those curves and covered little of her pale skin. Steffen had a memory that could hold on to images for years, even decades. What he did not bother about was names. Remembering names only made sense when you cared about a person. Random people were better handled as images.

"She's only a waitress at a café that overlooks our target's house," Steffen said, his voice sharp and reproachful. "Yet you make her sound special."

Tors's face fell and Steffen looked away, thoroughly repulsed. Tors was still too immature even to be an apprentice. Steffen often wondered if the idiot was cut out to be an assassin at all. He needed Tors though, especially during assignments like these. On his own, he stood out too much because of his implants. The perfectly normal Tors was the best person to handle interactions with the regular world while Steffen monitored his target. Only if Tors were more dependable, Steffen could have left the watching to him.

Maybe that's it. Maybe setting Tors free is the answer. What if...Yes!

He had to leave Tors alone with these observation exercises. The responsibility would do him good, teach him to think on his feet. Besides, watching a tubby old woman was a perfect assignment to start with.

"Here's our table, Master Pere." Tors pulled out a chair, eyes shining.

At least he got a good seat today. Steffen slipped into the chair and looked out the window. Across the street, there was a series of two-story row houses with pale blue roofs and curved stoops. Steffen fixed his gaze on the highest window of the leftmost unit. That was where the target spent most of her time. He could see her now, crouched in front of the windowsill. Reaching for the adjustment controls near his left ear, Steffen twiddled them a bit. The vision in his left eye changed, the telescoping function activating immediately.

"Some nectar for you, Master?" Tors asked, but Steffen hardly heard him. His eyes were fixed on the gray-haired woman who sat with a computing portal on one thigh and a fat cat on her other. She kept fidgeting, as if she were in pain. It had to be her hips. A smile twisted Steffen's lips. He could already see the end of this beat-up old woman. He'd be free of this vexing assignment soon. Very soon indeed.

FADE

Noell Rivans

Noell had difficulty believing two whole days had passed since they arrived in Ajokkan. Two days without having to fear. That was a lie, Noell corrected immediately. Fear was everywhere, lurking in the corners of her room, wrapped in the sound of unknown footsteps outside her door, and hidden in the darkness that shrouded the roads leading up to the tavern. The safety and the peace felt fragile, drifting, and too good to be true. Her children, four-year-old Eos and ten-month-old Jovan, played in the corner of the tiny room atop the alehouse, as if they had lived there forever. Their happy, rapturous laughter filled the room every now and then, making Noell's heart soar. Busily, she stirred the dough that would make their evening meal.

She had come looking for shelter. The only person she knew who would help was her uncle Arum. Everyone else — her parents, her brothers — would turn their backs on her. Raised almost in seclusion, in part due to the remoteness of her family's homestead, Noell did not have friends either. She had no one she could count on. No one who would dare stand up against her monster of a husband, Luca. Her family knew what Luca was up to, but they had looked the other way.

In the beginning, Noell could not understand the quiet and cold disinterest of her family. Their disregard of her plight hurt more than the blows Luca rained on her almost every other night. No one had ever taught her to fight back, so she took the beating with the quiet fortitude of a muzzled animal. She did write to her family, but they hardly wrote back. Her family's hesitation to intervene slowly dawned on her — annulling Noell's marriage within the first two years would mean returning the entire dowry Luca had paid for her. That was too much to give back.

With no choice but to continue living with Luca, Noell had counted days until the end of two years. Then, she was sure her family would invade Luca's house and storm away with her. In the eighteenth month of her marriage, Noell found out Eos was on the way.

There was no way out after that. Noell knew Luca would not give up his rights to a child and she was certain her parents would not want that battle on their hands. At nineteen, she was too young to take up the fight herself. Besides, she had no skills to speak of, nothing she could use to earn a living. She had never even been outside the Robben-Xiu system. Still, she thought of ways to escape Luca.

Noell remembered the morning when she seriously started pondering running away. Eos was getting big inside her and Noell often woke up early. She was out in the legume field, surrounded by faint traces of night moisture from the ground rising in a veil of mist around her. It left a cool, damp tingle on her skin.

"Miss Noell," said a soft voice. "Your breakfast is ready."

It was Riana, the newest maid in the house—and Luca's latest interest. Noell did not feel like speaking to her, or looking at her.

"Miss Noell?" Riana had called again.

"I heard you," Noell had snapped. She felt the girl shuffle backward a little. Was she afraid?

She had turned to look at Riana. Petite and dark, Riana was just like any other girl, except for her large, luminous brown eyes. Perhaps that was what Luca liked about her so much.

"Master is waiting for you on the back porch," Riana had said hesitantly, taking another step back from Noell.

"How old are you, Riana?"

"Fifteen."

"Where's your family?"

Riana had given a sad shake of her head. "Never known family, miss. They dumped me at an orphanage when I was days old."

Noell had held her breath. How could anyone do that to an

infant?

"The orphanage kicked me out when I turned fifteen. Old enough to work for your food now, they said. So . . . I've been roaming from one planet to another looking for work."

"It sounds — "

"Terrible. It is. I've gone for days without food. I get enough to eat here though. I hope you won't throw me out, miss. I don't mean . . . I . . . I . . ."

Noell had placed a reassuring hand on the girl's head. What was the point in hurting her? Luca would just find another girl.

"I won't throw you out, Riana," she had said. "Eat as much as you want."

Riana's words had stayed with her all day. If she left Luca, she would have to become just like Riana. Running from planet to planet looking for work, days without food, drawing unwanted attention from people like Luca — did she dare face all that?

No! It was an impossible dream. Besides, it was not just about her anymore, she would also have an infant to take care of.

That was when Noell gave up hope and gave in to fate. For a while, Luca relented also. He did not mind if dinner was saltier than he liked it to be, he did not fly into murderous rage when Noell accidentally cracked his favorite teacup. Even his wild and open trysts with the helping hands waned. But not for long. By the time Eos took her first steps, things were back to the old, unpleasant normal.

Noell's thoughts shattered in an instant at the sharp rap on the door. She froze momentarily before exhaling at the "It's me" that followed.

Eos jumped up, rushed to the door, and yanked it open even before Noell could blink. "Uncle Arum!" the little girl squealed, and threw herself on their green-haired visitor.

Arum was Noell's uncle, but Eos had taken to calling him uncle as well. And the man seemed to like it, so Noell let it be.

"All packed?" Arum asked. He picked up Jovan and looked

around the room.

"There's not much to pack," Noell replied. All she had was a couple of bags, mostly food for the children and a few of their clothes.

"Here's the place I told you about." Arum held out a square piece of paper with a picture on it. Noell barely had a glimpse of the place before Eos swooped on it, but the two-story building looked inviting with its warm, rust coloring and soaring entranceway. Thick, aesthetically placed vines crawled up the pillars along the stone path that led up to the metalwork door. It seemed nice, and Noell hoped it would be safe.

"It's beautiful," Eos gushed. "Is this where we'll live, Uncle Arum?"

Arum patted the girl's head and looked quizzically at Noell. "What do you think?" he asked. "Weimen Callum is an old friend. I trust him. He and his wife Bea have run this lodge for twenty years. They call it the Martian Hideaway."

"That's a funny name," Eos declared wisely, making Arum chuckle. "Do Martians hide there?"

Arum shrugged. "I have no idea. I do know the name's got something to do with his heritage. You have to ask him yourself. The man can tell a good tale."

"Are we going, Mama?" Eos asked.

Looking at her sparkling eyes, Noell wanted to say "yes" more than anything else, but she knew it had to be given a little more thought.

"Let me think about it, all right? Can you watch your brother for a bit?" She needed a moment with Arum. As soon as her daughter led Jovan away to their corner, Noell turned to her uncle.

"How far is it from here?"

"Across town," Arum replied. "It's far enough, I think."

"But . . ."

"What is it?"

"You said the owner is your friend."

"You think Luca will make the connection?"

Luca had a sixth sense. He was as smart as he was vicious — men like him always found out about things. It was a miracle that she was able to get out of Robben-Xiu without him knowing. She had planned for years — collecting bits and pieces of information from random people. Riana told her a lot about the freight ships that ferried people illegally between systems. She even told her who the shadiest freight ship captains were, and the money they demanded for such passage. Someone else, Noell could not remember who, had told her a story of how they had skimmed money from his employer for years. Noell took the advice, and slowly her secret stash of coins grew. She also stowed away outfits the poor maids and their children used. Perhaps someday she'd need them as disguise, she had thought.

It took not just years of such planning, but also a whole lot of luck — Luca being away at the legume farmers' gathering for two days, a neighbor inviting her for a stayover during that time, the two providing her with a head start and a cover — that helped her pull off this escape. Noell did not think that luck would last much longer.

"If he figures out I came to you . . ." Noell's voice dipped and her tongue grew heavy. "He'll find out where you sent me."

Arum's face tightened. He stared at the floorboards, his lips twisting into an angry scowl.

"You underestimate me, Noell," he said after a while. "I may be old, but . . . if that piece of rot comes to see me, he'll get what he has been asking for."

"You underestimate *him*, Uncle Arum," Noell said, but Arum looked away impatiently. Noell tugged his arm. "Listen, Uncle Arum. Luca is a dangerous man. Please don't do anything to — "

"We have to leave this place quickly then," Arum said. The way his eyes flashed and his cheeks reddened, Noell could tell he was irritated. "Weiman's place is safe, Noell," Arum said a moment later, sighing. "It's the safest place I can think of right now."

Noell nodded. That was true. Living in the alehouse where Uncle

Arum worked was not a sensible thing to do. She had to move away, quickly. And the Martian Hideaway seemed a good place for now. Later though, she would have to find a new place, a place where no one would know her at all.

ACQUIRE

Mako Nuyin

Mako's feet shook when he stepped on the dry, flaky soil of Robben-Xiu 4217. The heat was blistering, as if he had been placed inside a burning clay oven, but that was not what was making Mako miserable. He was miserable due to the flight.

All long-distance travel, particularly a trip like the one he had just made from Ajokkan to the southern fringes of the galaxy, necessitated the use of Fourian-mode. The Fourian, quite simply, was a drive capable of faster-than-light travel. It was the invention of the Fourian that made the Veloressian Empire possible in the first place, or at least helped the Empire reach as far as it did. Now, traveling across the galaxy, a half million light-years, was as commonplace as a breakfast of rolled bread and honey.

But traveling using Fourian-mode was harsh on the body, and for some people, like Mako, it wreaked havoc. Although he was not a soldier who needed to move between planets every few months, Mako could not altogether avoid interstellar travel. Every trip was torture. He tried many preventives — medicines, herbal concoctions to soothe his nerves, self-hypnosis — but nothing worked. It always came down to a stabilizing shot of Dexterone.

Mako opened his medical kit and pulled out a Dexterone capsule. He did not have much time on his hands. The instructions he received from the central office of the Imperial Intelligence Bureau were clear about one thing: wrap up the assignment as quickly as possible. Even though Mako still did not have details on the "bioreactor" he had been sent to retrieve, they had at least provided the location of the extraction site. Mako had dispatched a scout team from one of the Intelligence Bureau's local offices to stake out the site right away.

Now he wanted to reach the site and meet the scout team, but that demanded his nerves be stable. Mako pressed the Dexterone capsule over the cephalic vein. Another moment or two and the drug would do its trick by stabilizing his battered senses.

His deputy, Kerl Ogsen, strode up holding a minuscule computing portal that showed the location of their transport, the Deith, in blocky graphics. All around it was flat, barren land.

"Lieutenant," Kerl said, pointing at a red circle on the portal, "the extraction site is an hour's distance from here." It was due south of their current location. "I've asked Leyna and Brasi to get the Retriever ready."

Kerl being dependable, as always.

"All right," Mako said.

"We'll leave on your orders." Kerl, who knew of Mako's difficulties with the Fourian very well, strode away.

They were off soon, Kerl driving. The portal at the center of the Retriever — a ruggedized all-terrain vehicle invaluable on missions like these — beeped and the bronzed face of a curly haired man filled the screen.

"Scouting team reporting from site," the man said. "We see no disturbance. Except for one caretaker, the site seems empty."

"Good," Mako replied. The extraction would be simpler if there was only one caretaker to handle.

If only the central office had told us what we've been sent to extract.

But other than the coordinates of the site and the urgency of extracting the "bioreactor," Mako did not know much about the target.

"Hold position. We're less than an hour out."

The bright glare of the main star of the system, Robben, beat down on the road with impunity. All around, as far as the horizons, flat, chalky ground stretched endlessly. The road was empty, and except for one excavator and a container transport, Mako did not spot anything else during their long trek into Vell Rosen.

"Some place to live," Kerl commented drily when their Retriever pulled into the deep crease in the dusty ground that was Vell Rosen. "Valley of Roses — they named it right," he added sarcastically. The crease, although more of a gulch than a valley, offered some shelter from Robben's glare, and not letting the chance slip out of their hands, the 4217ers had put up homesteads all over. The buildings looked as inhospitable as the planet around them. Brown thatched silos, their sides plastered with mud, stood like petrified sentinels. Brown walls ringed the mostly barren courtyards. Every house seemed deserted; there was no sign of life anywhere.

"Looks like everyone is indoors," Leyna commented from the backseat.

Kerl nodded. "Robben is too hot this time of the day," he said. "People here work outside mostly in the early mornings. Or in the late afternoon. Or through the night."

"Good for us," Mako said.

"Yes," Kerl said between chuckles. "Pull an extraction in the middle of the day and no one's there to see. What could be better?"

The portal beeped, softly at first. Then the beep grew louder and more insistent.

"We're near," Mako said, straining to look for the site. It was supposedly the largest farm of Tollenbach legumes. Little plants that grew underneath the soil and produced a natural inhibitor against starlight burns, the Tollenbach legumes were precious. The Empire did not care much about the Closers — people desperate enough to inhabit planets so close to stars — but for these Closers, the Tollenbach legumes were a necessity for survival.

The plants were rare and they needed constant nurturing. They grew on all six inner planets of the Robben-Xiu system, but mostly on the 4217. People who could brave the punishing atmosphere of the planet were few though, like the homesteaders in Vell Rosen.

"Look at that." Brasi's voice was light with wonderment.

At the end of Vell Rosen was a homestead bigger than any they had seen until now. It sprawled on both side of the slopes, and the house, its roof painted a bright red, sat high up on the western edge. The sizeable yard was lined into rectangular blocks, which Mako deduced were patches of legume. Rows of pipes crisscrossed the yard as well, mirroring the pattern of the legume patches. At the entrance of the farm was a sign that read "Daksson's."

"That Daksson guy must be rich," Leyna said, "to have an irrigation system installed."

Mako checked the coordinates of the extraction site. It matched Daksson's farm. "That's our site."

The portal, which had been beeping shrilly as they drew closer to the farm, gave out a loud final beep before falling silent. The screen went dark when they reached the meeting point—in the comforting shadow of a large boulder—where the scout team was waiting.

"The central office hasn't transmitted the specs of the package yet," Mako said as he got off the Retriever, a bit annoyed at the needless delay. They could have sent the details long ago, but no, they decided to send them only after the team had reached the extraction site.

"Lazy, inefficient desk jockeys," Kerl said, scoffing.

Two men clad in brown stepped out from behind the boulder as soon as the whole team was on the ground.

"Ilyom, sir," the man in front, whose bronzed face Mako had seen on the Retriever's screen, announced. "And this is Bana."

"Good seeing," Mako said. "What have you got?"

"The farm seems empty. There's supposed to be a family of four living there: Luca Daksson, his wife, and two kids. Now there's only a caretaker, a woman, Azaki. She carries a long-barrel gun when she's outside, but she's just one person."

"The extraction should be easy then, right?" Kerl said. "Any challenges other than the caretaker?"

Ilyom and Bana shook their heads.

"Ready to go then?"

Mako's personal visor—a multipurpose eye shield the Intelligence

Bureau used to transmit confidential visual messages among other things — flickered to life as if on cue. Mako punched in the codes on his wrist-com and a picture flashed on the screen in an instant, making Mako blink in surprise.

It was a girl, a child of no more than five years. Her skin was the color of dark soil, her frizzy hair a shade or two darker than her skin, her eyes large and kind. A sizable mark shaped like a crescent moon slashed across the side of her forehead, perhaps the remnant of an injury that had healed some time ago.

Words flashed below the picture: "Specs for extraction mission — code name: Bioreactor; handle: Eos; age: 4; grade: Urgent and Classified."

"You received it?" Kerl asked, looking questioningly at Mako, who nodded with great difficulty. He could not fathom why anyone would want to have a four-year-old child extracted by a Special Ops team. Not that this was his first extraction — he had spied on and seized plenty of people in his decade-long career in the Special Ops, but most of them were deplorable, and their captures not hard to justify. But a four-year-old?

"What do you know about the family that lives on the farm?" Mako asked.

Ilyom looked startled at the question, and Mako did not miss the bewildered looks the rest of the team exchanged.

"Like I said, it's a family of four. According to the people of Vell Rosen, they're a happy family. Luca's wife's name is Noell; she's quite famous for her beauty. They have a four-year-old daughter, Eos, and an infant boy, Jovan."

"They left the farm?" Mako asked. Something else, something familiar stirred his memories, but he could not pin it down. His thoughts felt murky. *Damn the Fourian!*

"Yes," Ilyom said.

"When?"

"The mother and kids left a week ago, so we gathered from the other homesteaders. The father, Luca . . . we saw him leaving yesterday."

"Where did they go?"

Ilyom looked at Bana, and they both shrugged.

"Luca took a local transporter flight, so he must've gone to one of the inner planets here. No one knows where the rest of the family went."

"We've missed our target then," Mako said deliberately, watching faces around him freeze for an instant before wilting. This was their first failure in ten years as a team.

"You mean the target was one of the family members?" Leyna asked after a while, but Mako did not reply. Trustworthy as his crew was, Mako hesitated sharing the specs. Something about the assignment troubled him, but he was not sure what. He was distracted already, mind whirring in a frenzy. He patched in a hurried update to the central offices. It would take some time for the reply to arrive, so Mako decided to visit Luca Daksson's farm in the meantime.

"Let's go speak to the caretaker and check out the premises. No weapons — let's not spook anyone."

He had taken about twenty steps toward the legume farm when it hit him. Eos, the girl's name. He had heard it before. Roli had said that name. It was the girl the allegedly murdered oracle had spoken about. The girl with a mark of the moon on her forehead.

Could that girl be the same as my missing target?

CRACK

Bryanna Tu-Fei

Bryanna's fingertips, swollen and stiff, felt as if they had been pounded by a pestle. For three days straight she had clicked away at her portal, her fingers furious, as if possessed. She still had no idea of where the command to alter a public record had originated other than from one of the office rooms within the ODS's foundation, but she was sure she'd be able to find more if she tried. And try she did.

Bryanna analyzed the data one way and then another. She pored over all the information she had gathered over the years and fed it into the analysis. She programmed the computing portal over and over again to get to a conclusion about the origination point. Other than the fact that the command had been sent from one of the administrative offices of the Order of Divine Sight, she could deduce nothing else.

It had felt hopeless when she walked into Cognitivus the previous night. But now, heading out of the Cognitivus after her shift, she felt energized again. Her feet were still tired; she had slept little and skimped on meals over the last few days, but now she finally had what she thought was needed to crack the puzzle. She had more data. More stolen data, to be precise.

Unlike the data Bryanna had stolen the last time, this was not just live data but some from storage, which was far more risky. She could be executed for her crimes, or at least spend the rest of her life in prison.

Anything for the truth!

"Happy seeing," the guard at the entrance greeted Bryanna. "Have a good day."

There was something in his tone, a hint of wariness possibly, that made Bryanna stop and look at his face. She had never seen him before. His cap with the Cognitivus logo barely contained his fluffy yellow hair. He had a childish face and his mannerisms were stiff. It was as if he was no real guard, but was simply playing a part.

I'm thinking too much, Bryanna chided herself.

"It looks cold out there," Bryanna said, and the guard nodded.

"You're lucky. At least you don't have to walk far," he said just as Bryanna waved and walked out of the building. The cold gusts sweeping her face felt like icy nails scraping her skin. A few minutes out here and they would draw blood, Bryanna was sure. Thankfully, her house was only a stone's throw from the Cognitivus.

Even in the cold, the walk back home felt faster than it usually did. Picking up Nico in her arms, Bryanna filled the food and water bowls for the cats. Then, grabbing a bowl of food for herself, she settled onto her couch in front of the attic window. Arming the portal with the new set of data, she started her analysis.

She had decided on a new approach. She had tried enough with AC 20, the alteration command. Now she was going to dig into the record that had been tampered with by AC 20. So first, she separated all the records in her data set with the same origin codes as the altered record. There were hundreds and thousands of them. Next she tried to parse them based on the record type. And Bryanna had to slow down right away.

There were all sorts of records, many of them to the Prophecy Archives, many to various other administrative offices. Bryanna quickly extracted the ones that were sent to the Prophecy Archives just like the record she was investigating. She compared a set of those to the record in question, but found no apparent similarities. There was no pattern linking them; nothing jumped out at her like she had hoped.

Bryanna cradled her tired, throbbing head and sat still for a while. She was getting no further than she had been a day ago.

Did my robbery of data amount to nothing?

All the coding she thought she had mastered had resulted in this spectacular failure.

"Foolish old cat person," Bryanna muttered, her voice choking. "That's what you'll always be."

She had just reached for Nico with an exhausted arm when her other hand fell on the curved panel of keys. In a flash, her parsing program shut down and the data in its entirety — thousands of records sent to the archives — scrolled up the screen like an army of ants marching up the portal. Too tired and frustrated to even shut it off, Bryanna let the screen be.

"Your mother's not too bright after all, Nico," she said, sighing loudly. Nico simply looked up, vivid yellow eyes barely peeking through slits, and purred.

The data kept scrolling as Bryanna watched through blurry eyes. There went the tampered record she had flagged in red. There went another, similar in all respects to the flagged record. Then another. And another. They came in a nice little pattern, a securely wrapped data tag leading the way.

More of them flashed past — many of them cocooned within secure wraps just like her flagged record.

Wait! Bryanna sat up. *Is that really a pattern?*

She held her breath and waited for the next secure wrap.

There it was — another secure wrap, then a record with the same origin code and the same structure as the one she was scrutinizing. Each time, it was the same sequence.

She knew that secure records meant something. They were holding special information, they had to be . . . prophecies! These codes were meant to provide extra protection for the sensitive data of a prophecy while they traversed the electronic path to the Prophecy Archives.

And that meant someone had altered a prophecy!

No! It couldn't be! Not a prophecy! They couldn't have damaged a prophecy.

Bryanna blinked and leaned forward to look again. Nothing

changed. The parade of records streamed across the screen of her portal. The ones brandishing secure tags similar to the tampered record she was tracking seemed to flash brightly as they passed.

Each prophecy wrapped in the secure tags was followed by another codified field. Every one of them. Bryanna sat up as a thought hit her dazed brain.

Could that be a confirmation code?

Bryanna leaned forward and pulled up her spurned parsing program. Fingers clicking in a mad rush, she punched in some more instructions. The screen lit up with the pairs of records, matched in the expected pattern.

She looked closely at the confirmation record of each pair. The signature patterns in each of them matched exactly.

A nervous laughter left Bryanna's parched throat. There it was, clear as day. It was obvious—every prophecy automatically recorded in the Prophecy Archives was followed by a confirmation code that signified validation of the prophecy.

Every single one of them.

Except for one.

The one that was tampered with!

For this one prophecy that had been assailed by AC 20, there was no validation. Instead, someone sent a command to alter . . . no . . . more likely *wipe out* the transaction.

Bryanna sat there, blinking as she held her breath. She could not imagine the clear conclusion. Someone high up in the ranks of the ODS had not just tampered with a random record, they had possibly deleted a prophecy. It was unthinkable.

Only one person, Kianto had told her, had the authority to validate and confirm prophecies. It was always the head of the Order, which in this case meant Sister Paramount Magetha.

Bryanna fell back and closed her eyes. It *was* Magetha.

A faded memory surfaced in her dazed, sleep-deprived mind, one she had taught herself over the years to not obsess about. It was something Kianto had said about Magetha the last time he visited. Kianto had been sullen that day, bordering on depressed. It felt like he did not want to return to the ODS, and that was unusual. Like the hovering parent she was, Bryanna had pressed.

"What is it, Kianto? Don't you like your work?"

Kianto had looked up, startled.

"You're always so eager to get back to work," Bryanna had explained. "But not today."

"I-I . . ." Kianto stuttered. "I don't like what she's asking me to do."

"Who?"

"No one. Never mind." Kianto had rushed away. Within minutes, he had picked up his sack and set out for the ODS. His behavior had struck Bryanna as odd. Until that day, Bryanna had seen no questions, no hesitation, no lack of spirits in Kianto with regards to the ODS.

Yet Bryanna had brushed it off. Kianto respected the ODS, and Bryanna respected Kianto for his dedication to the ODS. Even though she wanted to, Bryanna did not pry when Kianto was secretive about his work at the Order. He had to be that way. Confidentiality was demanded of ODS personnel, particularly from people like Kianto, who worked closely with the chief supervisors of the organization. The boy was simply tired, she had thought.

Two days later, Kianto came back. He did not make it into the house. He'd died on the stairs, coughing up blood, as Bryanna held him and screamed for help.

Kianto worked for Magetha, who was yet to become Sister Paramount then. She was likely the woman Kianto had referred to, and Bryanna often wondered what she could've asked him to do. What if Kianto's reluctance to carry out orders had led to his falling out with someone powerful — and to his eventual murder?

What if . . . ?

Bryanna sat up hastily, gritting her teeth at the sharp pain in her hip. What if Magetha had forced Kianto to do something illegal, like messing with the prophecy records?

Yes! It had to be that. Maybe Bryanna did not have enough evidence to prove it, maybe all she had was a mother's instinct, but Bryanna had always suspected Magetha had something to do with Kianto's death. Now she had finally found some validation for her suspicions. If Magetha was brazen enough to alter a prophecy, would she think twice about murdering a lowly assistant like Kianto, who might have gotten in her way?

For an instant Bryanna's heart fluttered, hope of finding Kianto justice making her dizzy. In the next moment, tiredness swooped in and all Bryanna wanted was a good, long nap.

Magetha was far from being caught for her crimes. Finding out was only the first step. Now, faced with the immense knowledge of Sister Magetha's wrongdoing, Bryanna did not know what her next step could be. How could she prove that Magetha had deleted a prophecy? How could she ever bring the woman and the ODS to justice?

BETRAY

Mako Nuyin

"Come on, Mako. Eat something, for goodness' sake."

Orin's frustrated voice barely reached Mako. He was hunched over his food, groggy, exhausted, and hopeless.

"It's been three days since you got back from your mission," his father continued, "and you've hardly spoken. Or eaten. Or slept."

Mako stared guiltily at the fuzzy green pokal-grains Orin had painstakingly prepared for him. Scooping up a spoonful, he brought it to his mouth. Then, as the nausea hit his stomach in furious waves, he dropped the spoon.

"I can't, Father," he said. This was how it had been since he got back from the godforsaken desert lands on Robben-Xiu. The back-to-back Fourian-mode travel had sapped strength out of him.

"Let's go see a medic, then." Orin leaned over and peered at Mako's face with his worry-glazed, near-blind eyes. Mako shook his head; he knew what a medic would do. They would prescribe him a sleep drug and tell him to keep off Fourian-modes for a while. He could not stay away from work or stay off Fourians. Not now, with the war about to begin.

"This never happened to you before," Orin persisted. "Are you sure it's because of the Fourian-mode travel? It's not like you haven't used it before."

Mako often thought his father was bordering on senility, but the old man always surprised him with his keen observation skills. Orin could be sharp as a tack, just like now. Orin was correct; it was not just about the Fourian-mode travel.

It was about Roli's seeing Leon being killed. It was about the Order of Divine Sight lying about Leon. It was about being sent on a mission to find the girl — Eos — Leon had told Roli about before he died. There was something evil afoot, a conspiracy like nothing he had seen before, and the thought of it made the bottom of Mako's stomach crumble. And then the nausea rushed in.

Mako had to admit, unwillingly, that he was scared.

"You're not telling me something," Orin said accusingly. Crossing his arms, the old man glared at Mako.

"Are you sure Leon Courtee didn't reach you? Or the Order of · Divine Sight?" Mako asked.

Orin sat up straighter. "What's Leon got to do with this? Why do you keep asking about Leon?"

"It's nothing." Mako pushed his chair back and rose. Something vile was brewing, and getting his father into the muddle would not be prudent. Besides, Leon's family and his had been close, neighbors for some twenty or more years. Who knew how the old man would react to the news of Leon being dead? "I'll go take a walk. Don't wait up for me."

Mako shuffled out of the house, Orin's voice following him. "Don't go about drinking, you hear?"

"Don't worry, Father," Mako replied, pulling the jacket closer around him. In the last few days, the weather in Ajokkan had grown chilly. It drizzled every now and then, as was expected during the onset of winter. The dreary cold only made Mako more miserable.

On reaching the end of the Avenue of Marcessa, Mako stopped. The foundation buildings of the Order of Divine Sight were to the south. Standing here, Mako could see the burned-yellow curvature of their central, crescent-shaped monument. Mako stared in its direction, unable to decide. Leon had not reached out in four days, even after Mako had left him a message that should have been sure to kindle his curiosity. There were only two conclusions to reach from that: either Jacen, the Principal of Meetings at the ODS, had not given Leon the message or Leon was dead. Since Mako could not think why Jacen would refuse to pass the message to Leon, the other option seemed certain.

Oracle Prime Leon Courtee was dead, murdered by a man with metal implants.

Cold fingers tapped Mako's spine, making him shudder. Years ago, there had been whispers at the Intelligence Bureau — some said they were experimenting with cybernetics; some said they had discovered a way to resurrect dead people using metal infused with vitality serums. But like a million other top-secret projects at the Bureau, rumors were all there was, no evidence whatsoever of the existence of a cybernetics program. Then, slowly, the gossip faded as well and Mako forgot all about it, until now.

Was this metal man the result of such an experiment? But why did he kill Leon? Probably because Leon had found out about the faked prophecy. Question was: who had faked it, and why?

Mako breathed with all his might, letting the chilly afternoon air swirl through his lungs. He looked away from the crescent-shaped monument. There was no point visiting Jacen again. The oracle clusters were notoriously secretive, and if Jacen did not want to tell Mako that their lead oracle was missing five days ago, there was no reason he'd tell him now. It would only make them suspicious about Mako's intentions.

"Roli . . ." Mako muttered. "Have to find that boy and hear Leon's message again."

Problem was, Roli was a squatter. He could be anywhere in the tannery rows. The best way to find the boy was by finding Arum, the alemaster at Waterside. Determined, Mako headed in the northwest direction.

"Mako! Wait!" A shout assailed him barely a step and a half later.

Orin's stooped figure hobbled up to him.

"Father?"

"I'll come with you. I could use a walk too."

Mako knew why his father had rushed out after him, ignoring his stiff, swollen joints and fading eyesight. Orin was worried about his son and he was not about to let him out of his sight. Mako glanced at his father's puffed, out-of-breath face. Orin was too stubborn to be convinced otherwise, so Mako decided it would be better to let him tag along.

"Let me charter a streetcar."

"No, never." Orin raised an adamant hand. "I can still walk. We shall walk."

They set off, side by side, quietly. Thinking of Orin, Mako walked slower than usual. He had expected to be annoyed that the old man was slowing him down, but oddly, he felt at peace. This walk together was refreshing and nice.

"Where are we going?" Orin asked when they reached the grounds of the Prophecy Archives.

"To the Waterside Alehouse, on the other side of the tannery rows."

"Mako!" Orin burst out. "I told you. You shouldn't drink. Not in the state you're in now."

"I'm not," Mako reassured. "I'm going to talk to a man who works there. Arum, that's his name."

"Ah." His father sounded relieved. "Something to do with your spy work?"

"No," Mako replied. He wondered how much he could tell his father about Leon, then decided immediately that it was too risky to tell him anything. Mako found a fitting reply. "Just going to check on that boy Roli. See if he's all right."

"Oh, I see."

It took them a while to cross the grounds of the Archives. It was a week since the Eternity Prophecy had been delivered, and the whole city was decorated to commemorate the occasion. The Prophecy Archives were covered with lights, festoons, and paper lanterns. People, mostly sightseers from out of town, thronged the premises. A loud hum of excitement floated through the air.

When they had stepped onto the quiet, deserted road that led up to the tannery rows, Orin spoke. "Mako . . ." he started hesitantly.

"Yes?" Mako said.

"Something went wrong on this mission, didn't it?" Orin said, making Mako chuckle. His father was as observant as a hawk, he had to admit.

"It's nothing," he replied.

"You can talk to me without getting into specifics, you know," Orin said. "I'm not asking you to divulge spy secrets."

"I missed the target, Father," Mako blurted the disgraceful truth he had been trying his best to shackle in a closet in the dark depths of his mind. He felt light almost immediately, as if a million-roundel-weight had been lifted off him. "We reached too late."

"Ah."

"It wasn't my fault," Mako said angrily. "If they had told me what the target was instead of holding off until the last minute, I'd have tried something else."

"Those desk jockeys. Still incompetent."

"And then they wouldn't let me track the target," Mako grumbled. That was the part that riled him the most. He had offered to visit Robben-Xiu 4210, where the girl Eos's grandparents lived, but the central office had cut him off. "Return to Ajokkan," they had instructed.

"Why would they do that?"

"I don't know. Maybe they think I'm not good enough." The thought infuriated him. It was not his fault they'd missed the target. If local intel was correct, the target had left Robben-Xiu even before the case was assigned to Mako.

The girl—his target, Eos—bothered him also. Leon had mentioned that name. Mako wanted to believe that they were not one and the same, but a suspicion brewed darkly inside him. There was a chance, a good chance, that this was the same Eos Leon spoke of. If that was the case, then . . .

"Oh, come on, son." Orin patted his back reassuringly and Mako's thoughts scattered like leaves in autumn wind. "You haven't had a single failed mission in your career. This, even if it were your fault, which it wasn't, would be your first. And that cannot be a measure of incompetence. That's—"

"Unfair," Mako said. "That's what it is. They should've let me complete the mission instead of recalling me."

The recall was strange and unexpected. What's more, it was worrying. Failing this mission meant a missed wartime bounty, which was quite a loss. What if they benched him now for the duration of the war? That would mean a huge loss of earnings, not to mention the beating his career would take.

"Is that the alehouse?" Orin pointed at the forlorn building next to the edge of the musty lake. Mako nodded distractedly, wondering if Arum would be there.

A purple streetcar, orange ornamental designs covering its flanks, appeared from behind the alehouse as Mako and his father approached. The vehicle was full of passengers, and Mako could see their silhouettes through the open screens. As the vehicle drew closer, the back screens came down swiftly, but not before Mako caught a glimpse of Arum inside.

Mako waved. "Arum!"

The streetcar did not stop; it did not even slow down. Mako shouted, pulling his father out of the narrow road and away from the streetcar. Wind swept across his face—the air ripped apart by the car that became a blur before Mako could steady himself. His heart was thrashing relentlessly against his ribs, and in his grip Orin was shaking.

"Are you all right?" Mako asked his father.

"Your friend was in there?" Orin demanded, wheezing. "Are you sure it was him?"

Mako barely managed a whisper. "Yes, it was him all right."

Orin stared, his brows creeping upward on his forehead until they stopped and bunched into a knot. Nostrils flaring, Orin shook his head.

"What kind of friend is that? Why wouldn't he stop? And look how they drive these streetcars nowadays. Could've killed us."

Orin went on and on about recklessness and friendship and dwindling moralities, but Mako was hardly hearing him. His dazed brain was still trying to make sense of what he had just seen.

He had seen a young woman sitting next to Arum. And he could've sworn he had seen her before — in the cracked family portrait that sat in the alcove of the Daksson farmhouse.

Mako had been an agent at the Intelligence Bureau long enough to recognize a face after barely a glimpse. Her hair wasn't the rare red in the photograph, but her sharp cheekbones and the wide forehead were unmistakable, as was her intense gaze. He was sure the woman was none other than the mother of his missing target, Eos.

APPEAL

Noell Rivans

"Mama," Eos sobbed. The little girl, who had been overjoyed upon seeing the picture of the Martian Hideaway, had thrown an uncharacteristic tantrum on the day of the move.

Noell studied her daughter's rumpled face, and like always, her eyes lingered on the crescent-shaped mark on Eos's forehead, a reminder of Luca's murderous rage. Noell shuddered thinking of the night it had happened, when Luca had hit Eos with a harvesting hook and almost split the girl's head in half. Not even then had Eos cried this much. Not ever.

"What is it, Eos?" Noell wiped her daughter's tears and stroked her trembling chin for the hundredth time. She knew there would be no clear answer other than "I don't feel good," but maybe, Noell hoped, Eos would calm down a little.

They had reached the Martian Hideaway not too long ago. And just like Arum had said, Weimen and Bea Callum welcomed Noell and her children as if they were family. The room they gave her was everything Noell had wished for and more. Cozy and quiet, clean and tidy, the place brought Noell hope. She could start a new life here. If she could only get Eos to calm down.

"It's not . . . happy," Eos said, her breathing ragged.

"What's not happy?"

"I don't know." The girl jumped off her lap and ran to the corner behind the pale-blue sheeted bed.

Arum, who had lingered after the Callums had showed Noell her room, mostly because he was worried about Eos, walked over.

"Is she sick?" he asked.

"No, I don't think so."

"I haven't seen her like this before."

Noell shook her head in despair. "I haven't either. This isn't like her at all. She's scared, I think, that we'll be on our own."

"I'll wait a little," Arum declared, pulling up a chair.

Noell fidgeted. Arum looked tired. He had been through a lot already. All because of them. Arum was not getting any younger, and now in the dim light his age clearly showed. Noell noted the crinkled skin, the sallow cheeks, and the dark patches around his eyes.

"It's getting late, Uncle Arum," she said. "You have to go all the way across town."

"That's all right. I'm not going back to work anyway."

His eyes were restless. He was worried about something.

"Who was he, Uncle Arum?" she asked on a sudden hunch.

Arum looked at her sharply. "What do you mean?"

"The man. The one who called to you when we were leaving the alehouse."

Arum stared at her, holding her gaze steadily. "Why do you ask?"

"You've been very quiet since. Is he someone you fear?"

Arum chuckled and then shook his head. "No," he said, chuckling still. "He's a friend, Mako Nuyin. I trust him. Should've responded when he called. I—"

"Why didn't you?"

Arum massaged his forehead tenderly. "Didn't want anyone to know of you," he said, slowly rising to his feet.

Noell counted the floorboards. She'd imposed too much on Uncle Arum already. "I'm sorry."

Arum patted her cheek and turned to leave. "Don't worry, child. I'll speak to him tomorrow. I'll get going now."

He had nearly reached the door when Eos streaked across the room, meteor-like, and crashed into him. Clinging to Arum's legs like her life depended on it, she sobbed relentlessly.

"Eos." Noell firmly pulled her away. "You'll see him again soon. He has to go now. He has to travel far."

"Why can't he stay here, Mama?" Eos wailed. "Please, ask him to stay."

"We'll be fine, baby," Noell wrapped her arms around her daughter as Arum left. "Don't worry. Mama will take care of you."

HUNT

Bryanna Tu-Fei

It was almost midafternoon, and Bryanna prepared the day's meal hastily. She glanced for what seemed like the hundredth time at her personal portal sitting on the table next to her favorite couch near the attic window. On its screen, numbers and letters scrolled at a furious pace.

Bryanna tore her gaze away and started scooping out food for her cats. *I have to be patient,* Bryanna reminded herself. Before she could accuse the ODS and Sister Paramount Magetha, she had to be really sure. That was why she had to run the checks all over again. And that was precisely what she had instructed the portal to do.

It was now running a comparison between the tampered record and four other records — two of them prophecies cocooned in their secure tags, and two regular ones.

Plates all filled to the brim, Bryanna set them out, one at a time in a circle along the kitchen walls. Balls of fur streaked in and turned the room into a fuzz of happiness even before she was done setting down all twenty plates. Bryanna chuckled as she watched them eat — this was one scene that always made her thankful to be alive.

A shrill beep forced her to turn away. She hobbled toward the portal on seeing a bright "Tally Complete" message flash across the screen. Cradling the portal, she settled into her couch and started analyzing the data.

The first screen presented the results in large crisp letters: "No full match."

An invisible punch to her gut left Bryanna breathless. *What in the name of the Adi Niappan?* She had been sure the tampered record was a prophecy — it looked exactly like one, complete with secure tags. *Did I miss something?* She knew she must have, seeing that the comparison program did not agree with her conclusion. *But what can it be?*

Another tap and the next screen flashed, sharing more details of the check. A 90 percent match, it claimed, with the two prophecy records and 5 percent match with the regular ones.

At least the flagged record doesn't match the regular ones, Bryanna thought, somewhat relieved. She tapped again, eager to get to the details of divergences in pattern the program had detected.

Ever since Bryanna had stumbled across the alteration command and located the tampered record more than a week ago, she had been shocked by her discoveries over and over again. Now her mind had steeled somewhat, prepared to be stunned with even more dramatic revelations. Yet, she was not ready for the data that appeared on the next screen.

A graphical comparison sprawled across it, the tampered record sitting above the two other prophecy records. Large red arrows pointed at the differences between the three. Bryanna had expected to see an arrow point at the length of the records or something related to their content. And she was right—there was a note about the difference in length and the scrambling of the content, but it was another arrow that grabbed Bryanna's attention. It pointed at the secure tags at the end of the records.

"DOES NOT MATCH," screamed the words next to the arrow.

"How's that possible?" Bryanna muttered, her fingers tapping the portal's controls furiously to get deeper into specifics.

That information—the next level of particulars she wanted—was right there on the following screen. The comparison check showed the three secure tags side by side, with the tampered record's secure tag much bigger—about four times—than the other prophecy records she had used for the comparison.

Bryanna fell back into the couch and released the breath she'd been holding. *What did this mean?* They all had secure tags, so all of them had to be prophecies. But why would one prophecy be tagged with a larger code than the other?

Perhaps she was tired from the night shift, or perhaps her mind had been bombarded enough by the surprises that kept on coming, she did not know which for sure. But for a long time, Bryanna sat there with nothing on her mind but a fat chunk of blankness. Then the conclusion dawned on Bryanna, sluggishly, almost in slow motion. And it left her gaping, her shoulders sagging, and fingers numb as she took in the clear and unbelievable implication of her find.

The prophecy that was tagged with the larger code, the one that had been altered or possibly deleted, was clearly a prophecy more important than the thousand others.

Bryanna let her mind come to the conclusion at the pace of a snail, measuring every thought it took to get there, banishing the chance of a hasty and sinful inference. Yet, it still came to the one end Bryanna wanted to shun.

There was only one prophecy she knew fit the bill — one that was held higher than the rest in the Veloressian Empire, the sacred prophecy, and the one that the Empire considered second only to the Gods — the Eternity Prophecy.

Bryanna stared blankly at the screen until her vision blurred. Only then did she stir and blink. She rubbed her eyes as if to wipe clean what she had seen so far. Then, with a deep, bracing breath, she restarted the comparison program. Only this time, in addition to the tampered record, she included a thousand prophecy records that came before and after it. Then she let the portal be and walked away to give her growling stomach some respite.

She had barely cleaned the bowl of food when the portal finished its calculations and called for her. Bryanna was ready to be shocked. Yet her fingers shook and she forgot to breathe as she tapped the controls to read the new results.

If there were any doubts or questions left in Bryanna's mind, now they were washed away. The tampered record was unlike any other record that preceded or followed it.

Except one.

Just like Bryanna had expected. This other record that followed the tampered one was exactly alike — except for the confirmation code that came right after. While an alteration command had followed the tampered record, the other one had been successfully validated, like every other prophecy that was sent into the archives.

In that instant the fog lifted off Bryanna's mind and she clearly saw what had taken place. Someone, most likely Sister Paramount Magetha, had replaced one Eternity Prophecy with another.

No, that came out wrong, Bryanna told herself immediately.

The real truth was: Magetha had replaced the true Eternity Prophecy with a fake.

Bryanna shuddered. To think that Magetha could have faked the Eternity Prophecy! To think that the woman had paraded the fake prophecy at the Oracles' Conclave! To think that the whole Empire had been celebrating the fakery for a week!

Anger coiled thickly at the pit of Bryanna's stomach. How dare Magetha cheat the citizens of Veloressia of their most sacred belief?

For a moment, Bryanna wondered why Magetha had done it, but then rage swept the question away. It did not matter why, all that mattered was justice. Magetha had to pay for her crimes. And Bryanna was the only one who could make that happen.

She had to make Magetha pay.

Bryanna sat up straight, resolve steeling her tired muscles. Suddenly, it was about much more than getting justice for Kianto. This was about making things right for every citizen of the Empire. They needed her. The Empire needed her.

But she was just an old woman with a busted hip. How was she going to get justice? Sister Paramount Magetha and her ODS were strong, powerful, and immoral. If they could fake a prophecy, the Eternity Prophecy at that, they could do anything to keep their crime from being exposed. They could kill her and silence her forever.

Bryanna shuffled uneasily on her couch, trying in vain to find a comfortable position, the cogs in her brain whirring in frenzy.

Unmasking Magetha and the ODS could not be done in a straightforward way, Bryanna concluded. She could not simply walk into a constabulary and tell them about her findings. Who knew who was in on this conspiracy? They could lock her up for stealing data before anything and, knowing the nefarious ways of the ODS, Magetha and her cluster would simply find a way out.

How else can I do it, then?

Meow!

A bundle of softness jumped onto her lap, and for that moment Bryanna forgot the weighty task of exposing Magetha. She smiled at a purring Nico and wrapped her arms around the cat.

"Yes, we have to find a way," she whispered resolutely. A bright beam of sunlight broke through the clouds—a miraculous blessing from the Gods on the cold, blustery day. Bryanna hobbled over to the window, cradling Nico.

"Look, Nico, the sun's coming out," she cooed. Down below, the modest public garden in front of her house, with its sculptured fountain and manicured plants, shone and sparkled. On the pavement around it, people looked up at the sky. Among them was a man in brown walking into the tiny café. A burst of wind swept across and his hood slipped off his head, revealing fluffy yellow hair as bright as the sunshine. He was looking up, but not in the direction of the light. Instead, he was staring right at her windows.

Bryanna's heart skipped a beat.

Isn't that the guard from Cognitivus?

As she kept staring intently at the man, she suddenly remembered something else. The guard had said something about her house being close.

How did he know where I live? Has he been following me?

In that rush of clarity, Bryanna's heart almost stopped. She was not a fearful person, and she had never feared for her life. But now, when she had found the biggest reason to stay alive, an unexpected dread clenched her throat, choking her.

Bryanna quickly turned away from the window. She clutched Nico, ears straining to hear the reassuring thumping of his heart against hers. She tried to think. It was difficult to breathe. Her thoughts jumbled up, yet she knew for sure that someone had put her on their watch list.

Who could it be? The Cognitivus? Or was it the Order?

Did they already know she'd found out about Magetha? The bigger question was: what were they going to do with her now that she'd uncovered Magetha's secret?

ORDER

Steffen Pere

The cold and hazy light of daybreak spread like a spirit-sucking blanket over Ajokkan. Steffen hated days like these; they reminded him of the day Fia was taken.

Fia's laughter rang clear in his ears. Ten years had gone by and it did not make any difference. Thinking of her still made his heart flit like a feather, made his insides fall to pieces like paper turning to ashes. It was funny how he thought of his life in terms of Fia — before Fia, with Fia, and after Fia. He could close his eyes and there was Lissel, his beloved, large with their child. And then, in the next moment, he was fearfully holding this little bundle and a pink, crinkled face smiled toothlessly at him. In that instant, he had metamorphosed, changed forever from an ordinary clerk at the Imperial Intelligence Bureau to the king of the world.

Cold was the day when he saw her lifeless body lying in the park, a dark, damp halo of blood surrounding her tiny body riddled with holes.

My Fia! My little baby!

Steffen stopped. He had to drive that memory away before it took hold of him. There was no use thinking of her. Pining for her would not bring her back. Nothing would bring her back. Pushing his hood back a little, he breathed deep. The air, the moisture within it chilled into microscopic granules of ice, stung the part of Steffen's face that was still flesh.

He was alone on his walk today. Having Tors with him usually helped, but Steffen's patience was wearing thin. For three days they had observed the woman of the Cognitivus, and it was an ordeal tolerating Tors. The young man had too much joy — an emotion that did not befit an assassin's apprentice. He had to do something about it, make a man out of the boy.

Steffen walked past the sprawling foundation of an oracle cluster, lips curling in disgust. The Empire was not what it used to be. Rot had set in, and things were falling apart deep inside. The clusters had grown strong in the last decade, and they made no attempt to hide their growing power and affluence.

His eyes fell on a mangy dog near the expansive cast-iron gates. The mutt's ears were bitten off in places, its left eye was crusty, and fur had fallen off in patches. It walked with a pronounced limp and with its tail curled between its hind legs.

That dog would be happier dead.

Steffen's fingers stroked the smooth alabaster hilt of the laserglaive—a knife that could turn a man into a jarful of blood in a heartbeat—in his pocket.

A sharp trill buzzed in his head. "Master Pere." Tors, his voice a little shaky. "An Imperial summons."

Not again! Steffen drew a sharp breath, his jaw tightening. *What do they want now?*

For a moment, Steffen wanted to cut off the connection.

They can go to hell.

His life was once again spiraling into the depths of darkness and he did not like the stir of familiar old feelings—the uncontrollable urge to kill, the satisfying surge of power on seeing life ebb out of his victims, the need to keep the smell of blood lingering on his hands—inside him. He had pushed them out of his life, but now they were all back pulling him down again. All because of these random and unending elimination missions.

Why do they have to assign me these? He had killed plenty for them in the last ten years. Now he wanted to get away and get clean. Head the Bureau's Assassin Corps like he deserved.

If only they'd let me.

The Imperial Intelligence Bureau had brought him back from dead. And even though Fia's death tormented him every day, Steffen was still glad to be alive. How he could go about living, hiding his hideous lump of a body, breathing through lungs reinforced with metal mesh, killing people without a care, hoping to teach people his vicious ways, Steffen did not know. But he kept at it.

Back when he started working for the Intelligence Bureau, they sent him elimination lists of criminals who had, through legal loopholes or otherwise, escaped justice. Killing those lowlifes calmed Steffen. Knowing he was ridding the universe of foul individuals made him happy. It was as if he was saving Fia every day. In less than a year, it had become an addiction.

Besides, being alive and able to reminisce about the good times he had had with Fia and Lissel was a blessing. Steffen was content with his life.

That was why, Steffen reasoned, he was grateful to the Intelligence Bureau and patient with these new jobs.

"Patch it in," he said through gritted teeth. He strode closer to the walls of the foundation and rested his back against the rough, unyielding surface, ready to receive the summons.

The scroll with the Imperial insignia swamped his vision. Then the voice, mechanical and unrecognizable, filled his ears.

"Eliminate 426-YS-83080."

"Timeline?"

"Tonight."

"All right." That would be the end of watching the slobby cat person, as well as these annoying summonses.

"There's one more," the voice said.

Steffen's grasp on the knife tightened. One slash across the throat — that was what he wished to do to whomever was on the other end of the Imperial summons.

"This one's urgent," the voice droned on. "899-RX-92035."

RX? That meant a person born on another planet, not here in the Yimma Soren star system. Now they wanted him to travel out of Ajokkan on their never-ending quest? He *had* to protest this, no matter what the repercussions.

"I don't go outside—"

"Your target is in Ajokkan. We will send details on the target soon. Sending coordinates now."

Steffen recognized the flashing numbers. He knew that quarter across town all too well.

"Timeline?"

"This needs to close before Revelation Week commences."

Revelation Week, Steffen calculated quickly, was set to begin tomorrow, which meant he had less than a full day. This was an impossible ask. The woman of the Cognitivus had to be taken care of, and she could be only dispensed of when she walked back home from her shift in the morning. And this brand-new target needed studying, observing, before he could strike. There was not enough time to do both.

There was not enough time to object either, Steffen realized, as the communication channel clicked to an end.

Steffen waited there for a few minutes, for the fires of anger and the fog of disbelief in his brain to die down. Then the gears whirred, sparking ideas. He turned to look for the dog. It had coiled itself into one corner of the gates. With slow, deliberate steps, Steffen walked over to the creature and kneeled next to it.

Reaching for its flea-bitten head with his left hand, Steffen patted it. The dog looked up, startled. Its thin, dull-brown tail wagged slowly, and its mouth parted as if in a thankful smile. It was still smiling when Steffen's laserglaive came to rest at the base of its skull.

Steffen held the animal's head and stared at its watery brown eyes. One push of a button and they'd both have some peace. The mongrel's suffering would end, and seeing the blood would calm Steffen, let him think clearly again.

No! Steffen braced himself. *Not here.*

This would not befit the king that he was. They had made him stoop to killing dumpy women, but he could not start killing animals out in the open. That would be too low. With a pat on the animal's head, he rose to his feet.

Steffen resumed his walk, strides resolute and precise. With every step, his mind stilled and his thoughts arranged themselves in neat, perfectly logical stacks. He had to leave right away to locate this new target. Tors would have to handle the woman of Cognitivus.

Steffen breathed in a mighty heave, his lungs expanding with the expected mechanical groan. The air had warmed up a little. His steps quickened. There was no time to lose.

3

Order is nothing, but chaos is disguise.

—Adi Niappan of the great harvest

DISSONANCE

At the foundation buildings of the Order of Divine Sight, Sister Paramount Magetha's office chamber was the biggest, yet the simplest. The white-walled room was almost bare. A desk, its dark wooden surface polished like a mirror, gleamed even in the faintest light. A high-backed chair, Magetha's favorite, stood on one side of the table facing the door.

Precisely at midmorning, on the day leading up to Revelation Week, Sister Paramount Magetha glided into her chamber followed by a blue-robed woman whose outfit indicated a lower standing in the Order.

"You had questions, Sister Subordinate?" Magetha asked when she was seated, posture as rigid and straight as the chair under her. Her gaze, scanning the face of the woman who stood across the large desk, was cold, almost glacial.

"Yes, Sister Paramount," Xihin replied quickly, yet with no haste. She held Magetha's appraising gaze, seemingly without fear. "Our Oracle Prime has gone missing."

"Missing?" Magetha's brows shot up and a smile, contemptuous at best, curled her lips. "Who told you he is missing?"

"He has been absent from his scheduled sessions for over a week. He has not been seen on the foundation premises for just as long. I am the reporting supervisor, and I have not received a notice of absence, so I presume he is missing."

Sister Paramount Magetha shut a thick volume on her desk with unusual gusto and frowned at the woman.

"We at the Order do not *presume*, Sister Subordinate Xihin." She chewed the words and threw them out like cannon fire. "We do not jump to conclusions. We have faith in one another, and we ask our superiors for clarity when we cannot find it ourselves."

"That is why I am here, Sister Paramount," Xihin replied. The manner in which she smiled and pulled her shoulders together clearly expressed submission, almost a little too obviously to be natural. But it seemed to pacify Magetha, who waved her right hand immediately as if to clear the stiffness in the air.

"You are doing the right thing," she said. "Our Oracle Prime is absent for a reason—a reason no one knows about yet. He has been assigned to a task force for the Imperial Council, to lead our messengers into New Haphniss. I should have told you this before, but . . . I have been busy."

"War is certain, then?"

"Pray that it be, Xihin. Do you know how badly we need a war? We have not had one in fifty years. People are forgetting hardships, people are forgetting patriotism, and people are forgetting how to sacrifice for a cause. They are forgetting the path of righteousness. We are here to guide them, but they do not come seeking our help anymore. They do not need us, and that is not doing anyone good. A war will show people real adversity, true suffering. Only through suffering shall they see the light. They shall come to us."

Xihin stood, head bowed, lost in thought. Magetha continued, swept up in a trance of her own words.

"When war comes to New Haphniss, our messengers will be right there to show them the path to peace. Ours will be an honor like none other, and Leon Courtee is the luckiest among us all. He was chosen to lead the New Haphnissians into eternal peace."

Silence fell and, for a while, there was nothing but stillness. Then Xihin bowed low.

"Thank you for explaining, Sister Paramount. I am at peace now. My apologies for taking up your time."

"Always good seeing," Magetha replied, a content smile stretching her mouth wide. "Leon's assignment is to remain confidential, Sister Subordinate," she reminded Xihin snippily as she was about to leave the room. "I expect compliance without fail. From now on, there should be no discussion of Leon Courtee in the foundation."

Xihin left Magetha's chambers and hastily strode across the darkened corridors. She stopped only when she reached the large windows overlooking the foundation's inner courtyard. Grabbing the ornate balustrade tightly, Xihin breathed — in, out, in, out — like a fish yanked out of water desperate to make its gills work magic. It was a long while later that she uncurled her right fist, revealing a piece of parchment crumpled into a ball. Slowly, Xihin flattened it and brought it close to her face, as if making sure she had read every word correctly.

The handwriting was faded but still readable. The thick, chunky words held an accusation:

Magetha faked the Eternity Prophecy. Don't know why. Adi Niappan is a girl. Not from New Haphniss. Going to get proof now.
~Oracle Prime Courtee

The note was dated a week ago, but Xihin had only found it the previous night in one of her bureau drawers. Staring at it and recalling the lies she just heard from Magetha, Xihin shivered. She was sure the Oracle Prime was in trouble. Only she did not know how much trouble he was in or how she could help him.

HURT

Noell Rivans

The kitchen of the Martian Hideaway was a nightmare in yellow. The colors hit Noell like a punch in the abdomen, reminding her over and over again of something she desperately wanted to forget—her life on 4217. The walls were the soft glow of a rising Robben, as if it were just peeking up the horizon, and there was the blazing and fiery hue of it on the roof. The floor gave off the sunbaked afternoon ruddiness of 4217's deserts.

Noell struggled to keep her mind on the task she was assigned: preparing the vegetables for the meals. Her surroundings kept niggling her though, even more than not knowing why her daughter was throwing nonstop tantrums. The girl, along with her little brother, was staying up in their room while Noell worked. Thankfully, there was plenty of work and ample distraction. Revelation Week—a week of festivities to commemorate the founding of Adi Niappan's tenets thousands of years ago—was about to start the next day. There would be celebration and feasting, and the Martian Hideaway, just like any other eatery, was gearing up for imminent business.

Well after midmorning, Noell went up to the room to check on her children. Jovan was still napping peacefully in his makeshift cot, so Noell simply adjusted his covers a little before starting to look for her daughter. She found Eos behind the curtains, staring out the window that overlooked the back entrance of the Martian Hideaway. The girl's face was pale, her eyes wide and bulging, and her usually rosy lips quivered like a wilted leaf with some unnamed fear.

Noell pulled her daughter close. "Eos, you haven't even touched your food. What's going on?"

"I'm afraid," Eos replied simply.

Noell had heard that before. She only wished Eos could be more specific about what was frightening her. She was afraid to prod too much, so Noell wrapped her arms around Eos and rocked her.

The little girl almost melted into her bosom. For a while she lay there as quiet as a mouse. Then Eos looked up, tears streaming down her reddened face.

"I keep seeing thoughts, Mama," she whispered. "I want to stop, but I can't."

A chill coursed into Noell's heart and for a moment she could barely breathe, let alone reply. She had thought Eos was scared of the move, but what was she talking about? What did she mean by "seeing thoughts?"

Noell's own thoughts flew back to a year ago, the day Luca had erupted into a murderous rage and almost killed little Eos. The girl had been terrified that morning. She had kept telling Noell about her father being angry. Only Noell did not understand how Eos could know what her father was feeling, because Luca had left before daybreak to meet with some merchants at Pattain Doth, a trading post a half-day's journey across the sands. Little did she know that Luca was indeed angry. His crop of legumes had not fetched the price he had hoped, and he started smashing things the moment he set foot back in the house. He always did that when he was upset about anything. Only that day he did not even spare his child. Had Eos somehow foreseen her father's mad rampage? To this day, Noell did not know for sure.

"I keep thinking of Uncle Arum," Eos said between sobs, pulling Noell out of her memories.

Noell held her breath. For a moment, she was not just afraid to ask, but even afraid to think what the child might have seen. Whatever it was—Noell's petrified brain connected the dots slowly— it had upset the child immensely. It could not have been good.

Please, by the grace of the Adi Niappan, let Uncle Arum be all right, Noell prayed wordlessly as she stared at her daughter's face.

"Is Uncle Arum hurt in your thoughts?" Noell made herself utter the words she did not want to. But she had to help the child, no matter how it pained her.

"No," Eos replied, her tiny face twisting. "But I don't know."

Suddenly hopeful, Noell sat Eos up on her knees and looked into those doleful eyes.

"Eos," she whispered. "Tell me everything you're worried about. You have to. Maybe we can help Uncle Arum."

"I told you last night," Eos accused, her eyes filling with tears again. "I told you to stop Uncle Arum. I told you to make him stay."

Noell's first instinct was to retort, to tell Eos that she could not have known what her crying was about, but she stopped herself.

"I'm sorry, baby. Mama didn't understand," she said instead, wiping tears off her daughter's face. "But maybe it's not too late yet. Tell me."

Eos snuggled closer to Noell and stared listlessly out the window for a while.

"A shadow keeps following Uncle Arum," she said finally. "It is tall and . . . big."

"A shadow? You mean a person?"

"Maybe. He has a . . . stick."

"A what?"

"A long stick. Just like — "

Noell clamped her hand over the child's mouth. She did not want to hear what she knew Eos was about to say. A man with a stick, a man following Uncle Arum, and this feeling that left Eos distraught — it could only mean one thing. *He* was here. The monster she was running from — her husband Luca — had found them. Almost.

Uncle Arum!

Noell jumped up, and, dragging Eos by her arm, she rushed to Jovan's cot. She had bundled the infant and was about to dash out of the room with her children when she stopped.

What if I'm overreacting?

She was about to ask Weimen and Bea for help. Possibly scare them terribly.

What if it's for nothing?

Noell looked at her daughter. Eos clung to her leg, wide eyes studying Noell's face as she hesitated. There was fear in those eyes, and a plea. Eos needed someone to believe.

She's just a child. A frightened child. Anyone in her situation would have bad dreams. They could mean nothing.

Noell felt her daughter's grip on her leg tighten, as if Eos was trying to keep her from wavering. Noell's gaze traveled up Eos's face, coming to rest on the scar across her forehead. Thinking of the night it had happened always made her shudder. The blood . . . screams . . . a bottomless abyss inside her. Noell had not expected Eos to survive, but the little girl had pulled through. Noell recalled the first words out of her daughter's mouth when she came to the following morning: "Told you Papa would come home angry."

There was something about the girl. She *had* to believe her. Noell grabbed Eos's cold hand tightly and opened the door. She could not let Eos down again.

FIND

Mako Nuyin

If anyone could choose the one greatest thing about Mako Nuyin, they would have to pick his grit. Mako did not give up easily, and never if something bothered him or eluded him. In such cases, after sulking for a bit, the man pounced on the issue like a prodded and indignant reptile whose one instinct was to shred the disturbance to bits. Only then would he start to feel at ease.

On the morning after he had narrowly missed seeing Arum, Mako woke up in a particularly vengeful mood. He was done feeling sorry for himself and stewing over being wronged by the powers that be. Determined to take matters into his own hands, he decided to look for Arum.

Since his father would not let him set out alone unless he was sure Mako was feeling all right, Mako started by stuffing himself with every bit of breakfast he was served. He forced himself to eat three pieces of rolled bread and honey—the staple of Ajokkan—and then washed it down with a glass of juiced berries. Across the table from him, Orin had started to look pleased when Mako was halfway through.

It was close to midmorning when Mako reached the Waterside Alehouse. He left soon after with Arum's address in hand. The plan was simple: find Arum, ask him about the woman he was with, and take it from there. Mako knew Arum would not be able to deny the existence of the woman completely. That was because Mako had already found proof. It had been fairly easy; after only interviewing a third of the tavern's employees, one man recognized the picture of Eos's mother as the relative Arum had housed in one of the rooms above the alehouse.

Mako wondered, as he rushed northward from the tannery rows, why Arum denied a woman's presence upstairs the other night. And why didn't he stop the streetcar when Mako had called out for him the other day? Did he know of the extraction effort already? Or was it something else altogether?

Arum's house — an old, gray structure that looked stiff and steady in a boring sort of way — was a brief jaunt away from the alehouse. It did not, for even a moment, attract attention or feel inviting. The gray door matched the dull facade, as did the shutters on the windows. Like a typical low-income roundhouse, this one too was a bleak presence, Mako noted.

At the beat-up metal gate that led into the house, Mako paused for a moment to collect his thoughts. He had to be careful with his words, not only because this was a sensitive and confidential matter, but also because it was about Arum. The man was his friend, had been a sounding board for Mako over the years. Arum could not be browbeaten into spilling his secrets; he deserved respect.

Patches of untended grass, mostly browned and dead, covered the tiny yard surrounding the house. Mako strode briskly up the gravelly walkway that cut through it and, within ten steps, he stood at the front door of Arum's house.

There were no summoning bells. Mako looked around to make sure he was not missing anything before he knocked on the door. As he waited for Arum to answer, he thought of what he was going to say once again. He could not bring up the woman right away. How else could he begin then?

A gust of wind howled its way through the neighborhood, making Mako tug at his jacket. It was getting cold. *Some weather for Revelation Week,* Mako thought, frowning at the swiftly gathering clouds in the sky.

Why was it taking Arum so long to open the door?

Mako knocked again. He leaned closer to the door, straining to catch sounds inside. He thought he heard footsteps.

Roli! Mako remembered suddenly. *Yes, that has to be it.*

Roli was the right subject to begin the conversation with Arum. He could then steer it toward what the boy had seen and on to Eos.

"Open up, Arum," Mako muttered impatiently as he knocked for the third time. Was Arum away? It could not be. Arum's shift at the alehouse was in the evening and he often told Mako how he liked to rest his feet before the long hours at the bar. Besides, Mako was sure he'd heard shuffling feet inside. There was someone in there, he was certain.

Then why isn't he opening the door? Is he hiding the woman here?

Mako's eyes roamed to the shuttered windows. There was no way to look into the house as far as he could see. Unless . . .

Roundhouses like these usually had one door in the back, so after one last rap on the door, Mako decided to check the back side. With a quick look around, he ambled along the perimeter of the house, watching for any openings into the house as he walked.

The back side of the house was damp, the reason for which did not take long to figure out. A bog, overgrown trees surrounding it in thick darkness, lay right beyond the fenced backyard. The swamp was flooded, possibly due to the recent rains, and water overflowed into Arum's yard. Mako treaded slowly across the soft ground, steadily making his way toward the stooped back door.

He had almost reached the door when he noticed a movement among the trees surrounding the swamp. He stilled for a moment and squinted hard. It was dark out there, and Mako could not make out much, but he thought he saw a shadow move through the trees.

Can it be Arum? Mako stepped across the yard, trying to keep his eye on the swiftly disappearing silhouette of a person carrying a stick. *No, it could not be Arum.* This man was far too tall and too fast to be him. It had to be some random person, Mako thought, retracing his steps back to the stooped door.

There were no summoning bells near this door either. Mako rubbed his sore knuckles once before pounding the door as loudly as he could. Almost immediately, the door opened with a loud creak.

"Arum?" Mako called, cautiously stepping into the dark inside of the house. Careful as he was, he tripped against the leg of a table right away. "Yimma's flares!" Mako cursed loudly, wincing at the sharp pain in his toes. *This is getting ridiculous. Where the hell is Arum? Taking a nap?* It was almost time for his shift. This was no time for a nap, not for Arum anyway. According to the employees at the alehouse, Arum was never late. Ever.

In any case, it was not possible to look for the man in the house when he could not see a thing. Mako stumbled backward, feeling the wall next to the door for the light controls. He found them quickly. Mako was still flexing his toes to relieve the pain when he flipped the switches one by one. No light washed away the dark, not even a flicker came to life.

That was odd.

Mako stiffened the way he always stiffened right before the final charge in an extraction mission. There was no reason for the lights to be out, not in Ajokkan, not due to a natural cause. If the Empire was flooded with anything, it was energy. And every house in its reaches brimmed with energy supplies, in keeping with the promise of the first Adi Niappan. No household, particularly not in the capital city, should have a malfunctioning light. Every room was designed with three backup sources — if one failed, the next kicked in, and so on.

But evidently, not a single power source worked in Arum's house, and that was out of the ordinary, sinister even.

Mako patted his vest pockets. "Stupid me," he muttered angrily. He did not have the flashlight he always carried during missions, simply because he had not expected a casual trip to Arum's house to turn into a mission. He only had the Pontuvin, a projectile weapon he was licensed to carry as a Special Ops agent. Mako pulled it out, reached for the closed shutters of the one window in the room, and yanked them open.

Light, its hue tinged blue by the rays from Soren, seeped in. Mako took in his surroundings. He was in a sitting room, obvious from the chairs set around the low table at the center. The room was neatly arranged, not a thing out of place. On the other side of the sitting area, a door opened to the inner rooms. Mako headed toward that door, his gait measured and steady, Pontuvin ready in his hand, and ears on the alert for sounds.

Twenty steps across — that was Mako's estimate of the next room. He expected it to be darker since it was farther away from the door and the open window, but it was not entirely sightless. A glow came from one corner, not of a light, but something else. It took him a few moments to realize what it was — a com portal. So far, it was the only thing in this house that was powered up. That was even odder than the lights being out.

Pontuvin ready to shoot, Mako crossed the distance to the portal quickly. It was in slumber mode, a gray orb with the crested logo of the Empire at its center, spinning slowly on the screen. Mako tapped the orb and the screen brightened almost instantly.

"Four unread dispatches." A sharp, toneless voice ripped the deadly quiet. This portal, like all com portals, was a communication hub for the house. Mako recognized it as one of the newer models that controlled everything in the house — communication, ambience regulation, monitoring security systems.

Mako's hesitant finger hovered over the unread dispatches. No, he couldn't, he decided after a while. It was one thing demanding answers from Arum but quite another to go through his personal messages.

He was about to walk farther into the house when he heard the gurgle. It came from behind the large couch. It was indistinct, but Mako's combat-trained ears picked it up nonetheless.

There was no light in that area, so Mako used the portal as a flashlight. Cradling the unit so its glow was directed ahead of him, Mako peeped behind the couch. A man lay crumpled on the floor, stashed in the narrow space between the wall and the couch, drenched in blood.

"Arum!" Mako set the portal on the floor and hunched over him in an instant, his frantic fingers feeling for the pulse. It was faint and fading. Arum's face was covered in blood; a gash particularly foul spewed blood from the side of his forehead and covered his left eye completely.

Mako pulled up his wrist-com and punched the emergency code in a mad frenzy. There was a chance Arum could be saved. If only the crisis intervention team would arrive quickly enough!

He sat guard over Arum, Pontuvin steady in his right hand, his eyes glued on the portal. Perhaps when tugging the portal along, his hand had grazed over the unread dispatches. Now it played the opened message over and over again. It was from a woman he recognized quite easily—Eos's mother. She looked scared and worried.

"Leave the house, Uncle Arum," she said, voice choking. "He's here."

REGROUP

Steffen Pere

Never in his ten-year career as an Imperial assassin did Steffen feel so utterly out of control. Now, on the day before Revelation Week, saddled with two elimination requests and little time on his hands, fear of failure tried to raise its adamant head every few moments. He crushed it hastily, mightily also, but it kept coming back. Particularly when Tors trudged about, a wilted expression on his face in full and effective display, the flutter in Steffen's half-mechanical heart rose to an annoying murmur.

"Tors!" Steffen called his assistant into the room while he prepared to leave for the other side of town on his new quest. He had studied the sector around the coordinates he had been given, but they had not yet released the details of the target. Steffen still had hope that it would be a worthier assignment than an overweight oracle or a tubby woman with a busted hip.

"Yes, Master Pere?" Tors shuffled into the room. His spirit was just about gone, his eyes skimming the floor endlessly.

"What is it?" Steffen demanded, knowing well what it was. Tors was scared out of his wits. Over the years, he had helped Steffen dispose of his victims many times, but he had only ever killed once. That was a year ago, with Steffen by his side. Tors had put down an elderly man who was passed out in a dingy alley, a man who would not have survived that cold winter night anyway. Even then, Tors had taken it hard, much to Steffen's outrage.

However, today was different. And to his own disgust, Steffen felt for the boy. That was no way to train an assassin, Steffen knew. Yet he could not help himself.

"I fear that . . ." Tors's voice trailed off.

"Look me in the eye," Steffen hissed. "Behave like a master

assassin's worthy apprentice. People should fear you. They should shiver when you look at them. They should die out of fear long before you lay a finger on them."

Tors nodded vigorously, the yellow bushel of hair swayed and swished. "Yes, Master Pere."

"Stop shaking your head," Steffen growled. "What's your plan?"

Tors gulped noisily. "I'll go watch her now," he informed. "Then, when she ends her shift tomorrow, I'll be there."

"You'll follow her home?"

"Yes."

"What if she spots you?"

Tors's face brightened. "She will, of course."

Steffen squinted. Tors looked excited, and that was a good thing. A hopeful start at least.

"By the time she realizes what I intend to do to her, it'll be too late," Tors said, eyes sparkling. "If she understands at all. She looks quite dim to me."

"Never underestimate a target," Steffen barked a cautionary note, but he could not stop liking the sound of this confident Tors. Tors's plan, whatever it was, had to be good to have excited him. If Tors could get into the woman's house, she would be a breeze to eliminate. There would be no messed-up roads to clean, no accidental bystanders. It'd be a clean and simple mission.

"This is what I'll do, Master Pere," Tors started to explain, but Steffen held up his hand. He did not want to know everything. Tors had to plan things on his own, make split-moment decisions on his own, wrap things up on his own too. What he had heard was enough, and hearing any more would make Tors dependent on his counsel. He was already dependent enough.

"I don't want to know every detail," Steffen said. "Tell me when you get back after completing the mission."

Tors's eyes dimmed. "Yes, Master Pere."

"If you need a weapon, use the laserglaive," Steffen advised. "Go easy on the push. And clean up good."

Tors nodded again.

"I'll be on a mission until the morning, so don't patch any messages to me. Now leave."

As Tors shuffled out of the room, Steffen eased into the recharging station. It could be a long, difficult mission and he needed every part of him functioning at its best.

He was looking forward to an end to these tasks. This would be the last one, the summons had said. Or had it said that? Steffen could not recall clearly. Maybe that was simply a hope he cherished. In any case, Steffen had decided there could be no more missions after this. He would not accept any.

PLOT

Bryanna Tu-Fei

For a long while, fear sunk into Bryanna's heart, freezing her limbs and leaving her in an unthinking stupor. Then, just as suddenly as it had invaded her senses, the fear drained out. Once again, Bryanna's mind was back, sharp and quick as it thought and reasoned and planned and plotted.

Her first concern was the well-being of her cats. If anyone tried to break into her house and attack her, the cats, particularly Nico, would fight back, Bryanna was sure. Her babies could be hurt. She was not about to let them come in harm's way. So she hauled them, one or two at a time, to the animal sanctuary two street nodes away. The administrator there had turned from an acquaintance to a close friend over the years and Bryanna was able to find temporary shelter for all of her twenty darlings.

After that was taken care of, Bryanna thought of ways to ward off any possible intrusions. She was not strong, not in great physical shape either, so she'd have to use her brains to keep the yellow-haired man away. She would arm herself at home should he try to break in — a thick stick, a sharp knife, and some boiling water on the stove seemed good weapons. She buttressed the front door, moving a sturdy shoe rack against it. She soon realized the silliness of her plans.

True, her efforts would make a fortress of her home, but she could not stay holed up in the safety of her home forever. Sooner or later she would have to venture out — to see Nico and the rest of her brood, for her nightshift at the Cognitivus, and simply to carry on with her regular life.

What then?

The yellow-haired man could easily attack while she was out and about. Out there on the streets, Bryanna would not have a pot of boiling water to pour on her assailant. Sure, she could carry a knife or a stick, but how would that help? He would probably strike her dead before she even saw him, like assassins were supposed to do.

And what if he poisoned her? They must have used some sort of poison on Kianto, then why not her? Bryanna always cooked for herself, and now she could restrict her diet to whatever she had in her storage from months ago. But the water? She did not have that stockpiled. She had no choice but to use the regular supply lines, and those could be tampered with easily.

Bryanna walked over to the window overlooking the plaza and surveyed. There he was, sitting at the café across the road as expected, chatting with a waitress and drinking some muck they served.

Who is he? An enforcer of the Cognitivus? Or someone the Order of Divine Sight sent? Could he really be an assassin?

As a wave of dread coursed up her spine and sent chills throughout her body, Bryanna decided she had feared enough. Being afraid would not help her any. She had to fight the fear — and fight whoever had sent that stalker after her. She had to fight just like she had fought to save Nico, just like she had persisted in looking for evidence of wrongdoing at the ODS.

Shoving her portal into a rugged shoulder-sack, Bryanna pushed the shoe rack away and stomped out of her attic. She knew what she was going to do. First, she had to build a weapon, her kind of weapon, and then she had to find a way to use it. And all that she had to get done fairly quickly.

***

Bryanna had been Lillyan and Satyak Kosnaguri's education counselor when they were in preliminary school. Now, ten years later, the brother-sister duo were lanky teenagers, even brighter and sharper than they were as eight-year-olds.

Bryanna had kept in touch with them over the years. Not just because their exceptional talents had made a lasting impression on her and she wanted to know how far they'd go, but also because they had become her teachers over the years. The twins had helped her learn the language of machines, and even now, if she needed help with niggling codes, they were the first people she called on.

One thing Bryanna had never discussed with the twins: the mystery surrounding Kianto's death. They were too young when it happened, and even as the years passed and they grew from impetuous kids to dependable young adults, Bryanna did not invite them into her investigation of the Order of Divine Sight. To her, they were still little children, and it was not wise to pull a pair of kids into an ambiguous and illegal investigation into an organization as powerful as the ODS. Thinking about the danger she was in now, Bryanna was happy that she'd kept them out of it. But Bryanna also needed help with a related matter, and she could think of no one other than Lillyan and Satyak who could assist.

She took precautions leaving her house. The yellow-haired man could not know where she was going; he could not be allowed to connect her to Lillyan and Satyak. Bryanna already had a scheme in place, one she had used to transport her cats without the stalker finding out. Fifteen trips to the sanctuary had turned Bryanna into a master of sneaking out the back door, the one refuse collectors used to get into the row houses. It opened into a dim, lonely alley, but Bryanna picked the safest moment to sneak out—when the refuse van arrived to pick up the day's trash and blocked the view into the alley. Scuttling to the nearest street, she hailed a streetcar.

As the vehicle took off, Bryanna stole a quick look outside. No one was observing or following her as far as she could tell. The yellow-haired man, whom she had last observed sitting at the café across from her house, was nowhere to be seen. Relaxed and content, Bryanna let her head rest on the cushioned back of her seat. She had successfully slipped past her stalker.

When Bryanna's chartered streetcar dropped her off at the

sprawling Kosnaguri mansion in the affluent south-central section of Ajokkan, clouds were starting to crowd the far northern skies. Lurching across wide, paved walkways that led through the manicured lawns and shapely shrubs, Bryanna hurriedly tugged at the summoning bell next to the glossy front door carved all over with stylized scripts of ancient Veloressian.

A uniformed greeter opened the door, and a brief introduction later, he ushered Bryanna over the crystal-floored hallway inside and disappeared into one of the inner rooms. Looking at the soaring roof above, Bryanna was suddenly and painfully aware of her smallness. She tiptoed to one side, trying her best to keep her shoes from tinkling against the floor. She knew the Kosnaguris — independent traders who even owned a sizable fleet of starships — were wealthy, only she forgot to imagine how fancy their abode would be. This was a palace of sorts, the kind she had only read about.

"Counselor Bryanna!" The disbelieving shout reverberated across the vaulted roofs and warmed Bryanna's heart immediately. Hair flying, arms stretched wide, eighteen-year-old Lillyan almost skidded across the hallway and wrapped Bryanna into a tight hug. "What happened to you? You haven't called in weeks," she said.

Bryanna chuckled, noting how quickly the concern in her voice turned into a grudging complaint.

"Thought you'd forgotten us. Wouldn't be the first one to," Satyak grumbled as he walked in.

Bryanna's heart twitched. It had been like that since she'd met them ten years ago. She still remembered the note that was attached to their case file: "Parents unable to provide necessary guidance." Children with intelligence levels as high as theirs required engaged parenting. For the Kosnaguri twins, there was barely any parenting at all. The twins craved their parents' attention and time, both of which were scarce. Ten years later, Bryanna still saw the void in their eyes, albeit more concealed, but there nonetheless.

Bryanna patted Satyak's shoulders, hoping the frown on his face would ease. "I'm sorry. I would never forget you. I'm just getting a little old, that's all. Pains and aches take up too much time nowadays. More than I'd like them to."

Satyak grunted in response.

"That's all right." Lillyan sounded more forgiving. "Come inside. This is the first time you've visited."

***

Bryanna took a streetcar directly to the Cognitivus that evening. With the cats at the sanctuary, there was no reason to return home. She walked in expecting the yellow-haired man at the entrance, but Tio, the guard who reminded her of Kianto, sat there instead.

"Good seeing," Tio greeted, smiling warmly.

"Good seeing."

"Early tonight?"

Bryanna flashed a smile. *Indeed.*

She *was* early. The twins had handed her a tiny capsule filled with data that would help her reveal Magetha's tampering of records at the Prophecy Archives, and Bryanna was anxious to get to work.

"Revelation Week has everyone in a fluster," Bryanna said, rushing to complete the daily registration protocol. She decided to keep on talking, hoping Tio would not ask about the shoulder-sack she was carrying. Her personal portal was inside it and Cognitivus often raised a storm over bringing personal portals onto the premises. "I was worried about being late, seeing the crowds everywhere. Ended up being early instead."

Tio chuckled loudly. "Yes, it's a blessed week. We don't always get the chance of honoring Revelation Week together with a new Eternity Prophecy."

Bryanna stepped away from Tio's desk.

"Ah, yes. Blessed week indeed," she said, backing into the elevator. "Have a pleasant night."

The elevator door slowly twisted into place, wiping the view of Tio at his desk. Soon Bryanna was at her floor, its darkened expanse beckoning her with its reassuring familiarity. With a deep breath, Bryanna headed toward her desk. This was going to be a long and eventful night.

DREAD

Noell Rivans

Nothing seemed real anymore. Everything was a blur of disbelief and fear. Bea and Weimen were talking, but Noell could not tell what they were saying. All she heard was a dull, indistinct hum. Eos sat next to her and rocked back and forth, back and forth. On Noell's other side a com portal stood, its screen darkened. She was not waiting for it to light up, yet she stared at it, unblinking, barely even knowing what she was expecting.

Uncle Arum was not about to call her back.

If what Eos had felt was right, Luca was here in Ajokkan. Dread, lumps of it, crowded her throat and made breathing difficult. It also would not let her think. This was what always happened when she thought of Luca—she froze.

How did he manage to follow us here so quickly? My parents! They would have gladly told him of Uncle Arum.

A hand touched her cheek, and Noell shivered. "Renna?" Bea called. That was her fake name, Noell remembered. "You haven't told us yet. What are you so worried about?"

"Uncle Arum," Noell whispered. "I'm worried about him."

Bea sat down next to her and slipped an arm over her shoulder. "What about Uncle Arum?"

"He might be in danger. He might hurt Uncle Arum."

"Who are you talking about? Who's 'he'?" Bea leaned forward to look at her face. "I don't understand what you're saying."

Weimen stepped closer. "Renna, you left Arum a dispatch. Asked him to leave his house. Why?"

She should have told them. Bea and Weimen looked at her, their faces unguarded, unprepared. She should not have kept her past a secret from the people who were providing her refuge. If anything were to happen to them because of her, it would be unforgivable.

But how could she tell them? Hers was a shameful secret.

It's not your fault, she reminded herself immediately.

It was never her fault. Yet why did it always feel like she was to blame? Why couldn't she look them in the eye and tell them the truth?

"Renna, tell us," Bea goaded again.

Tell them?

"Mama." Eos wrapped her little arms around Noell's.

There was still time.

"My name is not Renna," Noell blurted. She saw surprise coursing through their faces, some fear as well, but she kept on speaking. She *had* to tell them while her courage lasted. "My real name is Noell. And I'm hiding from my husband, Luca."

LOCATE

Mako Nuyin

Mako walked out of Arum's house while the crisis intervention team was still securing the scene. They had already transported Arum — alive, but in critical condition — to the nearest triage center. Mako had lingered awhile, first to try to speak to Arum, but the man stayed unconscious. Since that route of inquiry was closed, Mako decided to study the dispatch.

The woman — Eos's mother — had sent the message from a well-lit room. There was nothing noteworthy about the place except for its bright yellow walls and a stack of utensils peeking on her left. There was one more thing — a steady, dull buzz in the background. And that was all.

A deluge of questions swamped Mako, and he could find answers to none. When he left Arum's house, questions battered his brain incessantly. Who had attacked Arum? And why? Obviously, the woman in the dispatch knew Arum was in danger and had wanted him to leave. It had to be someone they both knew. Who? Was it another extraction team the Intelligence Bureau had dispatched to get the girl?

A sharp tingle at his wrist jolted Mako out of his thoughts. His wrist-com was buzzing. His deputy Kerl's face was flashing on it. *That was quick!* Mako had extracted some data from Arum's com portal and sent it over to Kerl for analysis. He had hoped that Kerl would find some information on the dispatch, maybe some clue to where it had originated.

"Mako," Kerl's voice streamed into Mako's ears when he routed the dispatch into his earpiece. "I got the origin coordinates. But you have to understand, they only give a rough location."

Mako knew that. Origination codes for voice dispatches could not be pinpointed to an exact location. But still, it was something.

"I know," he said. "Send them over."

Numbers flashed on his wrist-com. Mako overlaid the coordinates on a map of Ajokkan and a location lit up like a beacon. It was a spot across town, in the middle of Rookvig Circle, a section famous for its eateries. The stack of utensils he had noticed in the dispatch made perfect sense now — the woman had been speaking from an eatery.

"Mako," Kerl's voice sounded again. "What's this about?"

Mako had not sent Kerl the entire dispatch, so he could not make the connection to the woman. Now Mako wondered how much he could tell his deputy.

"Just a favor I'm doing for a friend," he said. Guess he did not want to share much with Kerl after all. "He needs a call traced. Thanks, Kerl."

"Anytime. See you soon."

"See you." Mako ended the dispatch, a wry smile curling his lips. The way things were going, Mako did not know if he was going to see anyone soon. Things were starting to look dreadfully complicated.

***

When Mako reached Rookvig Circle, daylight was past its peak glory. Crowds were starting to form on the boulevards lined with eateries of various sorts. Using the approximate location Kerl had sent, Mako headed to the northern end of the locality. He still did not know how he would locate the woman in the dispatch, but as he walked across Rookvig Circle, his steps were buoyant with pride.

For one, he had found his quarry — the one the central office had snatched away from him. *Take that!* Satisfaction apart, he was also curious about the little girl. He still wanted to scoff at the absurdity of Leon's claim. No one could have the audacity of faking a prophecy, let alone the Eternity Prophecy. But Leon had gone missing, was possibly murdered. If he could believe that, why would faking the Eternity

Prophecy be absurd at all?

Now, if someone *had* faked the prophecy, then this girl would have to be the next Holy One, the next Adi Niappan. Mako shook his head. This he could not believe. *What a ridiculous thought,* he chuckled softly. *A holy girl? Ludicrous at best.*

But then . . . he slowed as thoughts twisted in knotted circles in his mind. Everything had been a little bizarre since the Eternity Prophecy was announced. Leon's disappearance, his own strange assignment to Robben-Xiu, and now the assault on Arum — nothing made sense. As if someone had shuffled the world he knew and tossed the pieces up in the air. But if he accepted the weirdest truth, the one about the girl . . .

Did everything fall into place then?

What if everything else was a reaction to that one extreme and unbelievable truth?

A sharp and distracting buzz rattled the air. Annoyed by the ear-piercing monotone, Mako looked for the source of the noise and located it immediately. It came from a formidable hoisted winch, hanging high above the roads of Rookvig Circle. The machine was drilling a hole; Mako could tell from the sound and the tools attached to its curved nose.

The nausea that had lingered from the Fourian-mode rushed back at the continuing hum of the drill. Mako stopped to catch his breath. This was getting hard. He did not even know which of these buildings the woman had called from, and with the noise churning his insides mercilessly, there was little chance he could look for clues in peace. Mako sat down on a bench and, clamping his hands over his ears, he waited for the machine's digging cycle to finish.

He could not wait that long. Something else, a piece of memory, made him forget his discomfort and sit up. That buzz — he had heard that before. He had heard that in the background as Eos's mother sent the dispatch to Arum. That meant he was close to the place from where she had sent it.

Mako scanned the area in a rush. There were three eateries in the near vicinity. The largest—a blue-and-white, three-story monstrosity—was closest to where he stood. "Burlos's," a gaudy pink banner screamed. Next to it was "Watching the Waves," an establishment mimicking the ocean side, complete with thatched huts and a sandy floor. That had to be the location, Mako reasoned, the likely place with walls painted yellow to emulate the brightness of coastal days.

He set off in a hurry but came back out of Watching the Waves not too long after, his spirited steps turned into a lifeless slog. All its walls, the ones Mako could see anyway, were blue. Moreover, no one knew of a little girl and her mother. No one, not even the proprietor who'd rushed to intercept the strange man barging into the kitchen, knew Arum either.

The drill was silent for the moment, but Mako's stomach still churned. He looked left and right, trying to decide. Burlos's was right next door. The third eatery, a rust-colored building with a stone walkway, was a distance away. It had to be one of these two. Daylight was starting to fade, and Mako did not want to stretch his search into the night. He decided to try the one in the distance first.

***

"Who are you looking for?"

Weimen Callum, the proud owner of the Martian Hideaway, was as eccentric as the name he had bestowed on his eatery. He wore a patchwork robe that was the current trend in Ajokkan; his light brown-and-gray dreadlocked hair swished and swirled around his face when he talked, sometimes revealing the ring on his left ear—the largest ring Mako had ever seen on a man.

The greeter who'd answered the door had left to fetch Weimen as soon as Mako had mentioned a little girl and Arum, an action that made the churn in Mako's gut subside a bit. There was even a flutter of joy.

I'm going to show them that Mako Nuyin is the best in the Ops; there'll be no benching me and my team.

He could even demand the promised bounty if he chose to. The jingling of a beaded partition interrupted his musing, and Weimen Callum had appeared.

Now Weimen, resplendent in his multicolored robe, studied Mako intently as he waited for an answer.

"I'm a friend of Arum's," Mako replied, knowing that was not the answer the man was seeking. But he surmised it would more than suffice. And it did.

The moment Mako mentioned Arum, the man's face tightened.

"How do you know Arum?"

"I like to visit the Waterside Alehouse," Mako said truthfully, watching the play of emotions in Weimen's eyes. "Been going there for about ten years, had to be friends with the man who makes the best bitters in Ajokkan."

Weimen's eyebrow shot up. "What's your favorite of his?"

"Dead Mutt."

Weimen chuckled loudly. It was a quiet confirmation that Mako indeed knew Arum. Dead Mutt was one of Arum's signature mixes, and very few knew that it existed. It was an offering reserved only for Arum's closest friends and favored customers.

"Mine too," Weimen said, nodding thoughtfully. His eyes hardened momentarily. "Why are you here?"

Mako did not have to think twice. "Someone tried to kill Arum."

The girl shot out from beyond the partition, a tiny frame topped with bouncy curls, her eyes straining. The large, crescent-shaped mark across her forehead was a sullen reminder of some painful injury.

"Have you seen my Uncle Arum?" she demanded, but Mako barely heard. He barely even breathed.

The mark! It's the mark of the moon. Just like Leon had said.

"You've seen him, haven't you?" she asked again.

Mako knew she was four, yet she looked so wise. She also looked sad, as if she cradled the suffering of the universe in her heart.

"Have you seen Uncle Arum?" It was only after her mother repeated the question that Mako heard it. The woman he had been chasing was standing in front of him, holding an infant. Behind her stood an older woman, perhaps the owner's wife — guessing by the way she exchanged looks with Weimen.

"Yes, I found him," Mako said, halting over his words. He did not know how much he could say in the presence of the little girl.

Eos was her name, Leon had told Roli. She, with the mark of the moon across her forehead, was the one of the prophecy.

"You can say it," her mother insisted. "Eos knows Uncle Arum is in danger. She was the one who knew. She saw Luca go after Uncle Arum."

Mako peeled his appraising glance away from the girl's face and turned toward her mother. "He's still alive, but . . . someone attacked him. Hit him in the head with something heavy."

"It's Luca."

Mako remembered that name. Luca Daksson was the target's father, Eos's father. He was the richest legume farmer on 4217, with the largest farm on that desiccated planet. The question was: why would Luca hurt Arum so badly? Why would he hurt Arum at all?

Before he could ask, the older woman, Bea, gasped and turned her disbelieving gaze on Eos's mother. "Are you sure, Noell? Arum's old and . . . he's family. Your husband would hurt him like that?"

"Luca can do anything," Noell said, sighing as she pulled Eos close. She tilted the little girl's face toward the light. "He did this to her, his own child. Nearly killed her. All because he didn't get a good price for his crop. He has a . . . temper."

"Why is he angry with Arum?" Mako asked.

"Because we left him." Eos's little voice, clear and melodious, tinkled. "And because Uncle Arum helped us hide."

"No one else would help us," Noell added. Her eyes, large like her daughter's but a deeper shade of amber, brimmed with tears. "Except Uncle Arum."

Mako almost shook his head. This complicated matters even more. On top of the faked prophecy and the Intelligence Bureau hunting the girl, there was a father on a murderous rampage.

"We have to leave," Noell said. She held Bea's hand and looked pleadingly at her. "We have to leave before he gets here and hurts any of you."

"He wouldn't come here," Bea protested. "How would he know you're here?"

"The same way this man found out."

Mako bristled at her casual reference to him. Finding them was not easy. And he was not just any man. It would not be so easy for the husband to get here. But then, Luca could have help. He could've also gotten information out of Arum.

"There's a possibility," Mako said.

"Can you take us away from here, please?" said a little voice.

Mako glanced at the girl tugging his leg and struggled to tear his gaze away from the mark on her forehead. They were not his responsibility. On the other hand, if he could bring the girl in and complete his mission . . .

What am I thinking?

Leon died for his vision of this girl. Arum almost got killed trying to help her.

The signs are clear. Yet I'm about to hesitate? And even if she's not the Holy One, she's a child. How could I think of bringing her in?

There was no reason for shame. Mako collected himself quickly. She was a mission, and no different from any other.

"Aren't you going to help us?"

That voice again. So clear that it passed through his soul and washed it clean. So full of music that it reminded him of a spring morning. How could a girl so small sway him so easily? Mako did not want to look into her spellbinding eyes. Yet he did.

"Yes," he said, smiling at Eos. "Of course I will."

He *had* to help them. He had to respect Leon's faith in him, as well as Arum's hope of protecting them. And this family needed someone capable enough to keep them safe.

Somewhere deep inside, Mako knew something more. There was something about this girl. It was not just the murderous father who was following them. It was more. No one had called off the extraction; a team would definitely come to take this girl away eventually.

Mako had no doubt that Leon had seen the truth. The little girl who clung to her mother's leg and flashed a grateful smile at him was indeed the answer the Empire had been seeking.

STUDY

Steffen Pere

Steffen despised Rookvig Circle. The last thing he wanted to do was spend an entire day in the area. Sights and sounds of this lively section of Ajokkan crawled under his skin and clawed doggedly at the memories he kept stashed away in the far corner of his brain. He only let them out in the confines of his home — not when he was out in the world, and never when he was out pursuing his prey. But today was different. There was no other way; he had to be here to keep watch on his target, and the memories were winning.

Why did they have to send me here?

Steffen wished Tors were with him. The bigmouth would've kept him annoyed enough to stop him from drifting into thoughts that did no good.

Fia was gone. Forever. And there was no amount of wishing or dreaming that would bring his baby girl back, Steffen knew that. If only knowing could help.

Ten years had passed, but Fia did not fade. Every memory had only grown stronger. Being in Rookvig Circle, two nodes away from Fia's favorite fruits-and-cream shop, only made the anguish stronger.

Thinking of Fia was wrong. He had to stop it. The only way to get his focus back was to get into the mode. He needed to see blood . . . soak his hands in it and fill his lungs with its sharp, tangy odor. But it was broad daylight, and he could not kill anyone out here no matter how badly he wanted it.

Steffen closed his eyes and breathed, nose curling in annoyance when the aroma of roasted pokal-grains drifted through the air. Another distraction: the food. Fia's mother, Lissel, loved coming here to try the newest and the trendiest eateries, and she surely passed on her love of food to her daughter. And later, even when Lissel was away on a prolonged tour of duty like any other Imperial soldier and her absence pained Steffen, he brought Fia to Rookvig Circle every week. Coming here was almost homage to the woman father and daughter missed so badly. Slowly, they had created their very own "Ritual of the Rookvig," as Lissel used to call it.

Steffen writhed in discomfort. This was a mistake. He should have refused this assignment. He should have known this would bring back too many memories. Grunting loudly, he rose from his hiding spot between two oversize ardelbushes, brushing off their short, prickly leaves from his clothes. He had watched the Martian Hideaway for too long. Since he could not do much more until he had information on the target, Steffen decided to stretch his limbs a little. The metal joints needed moving from time to time or they stuck, and always in the rottenest of times.

As evening drew closer, people—dressed in overelaborate and grating finery—started crowding the streets. *It's getting harder to keep watch,* Steffen thought angrily. Soon there would be even more people on the streets and even less light. And the senseless person sending these summonses had not patched him the details of his target yet. All Steffen had was an identity code. Didn't they know identity codes were useless? Those numbers weren't exactly printed across people's foreheads. He needed visual confirmation of whomever they had sent him to eliminate. It was getting darker and he still had nothing.

He had crawled back into his makeshift furrow between the ardelbushes when he noticed the man walk into the Martian Hideaway. He was dressed in black, his dark, longish hair disgustingly scruffy. Even from this distance, Steffen could tell the man had not slept well in days.

Something about him vexed Steffen. Perhaps it was the way he scanned the roads before entering the gates of the eatery, just like a man trained in covert operations would do. Or perhaps it was his gait—a grace born out of practiced stealth oozing from each step. This man, Steffen was sure, was not an ordinary Veloressian. Why was this man at the Martian Hideaway? Steffen craved for an answer, knowing well that none was coming. There was little Master Assassin Steffen Pere could do at the moment but wait.

So, Steffen thought about Tors instead. Just a boy when he was named to assist him, Tors had adjusted to Steffen's daily regimen quite easily. Steffen had half-expected the boy to break under pressure, but he had not. It had to be hard living with the killing machine that Steffen had turned into, yet the boy grew into a man with cheer on his face.

I don't praise Tors enough these days, Steffen thought before he rebuked himself once again.

Praise and pampering did not befit their profession. Tors needed toughening up, not coddling. How could he, Master Assassin Steffen Pere, think like a soft-bellied apprentice? Had to be the effect of this place.

I'm losing my mind. I need to get out of here.

Steffen scrambled out of his hiding spot once more and paced furiously. He checked his com port.

Maybe Tors messed up the dispatch system.

What could be the reason for the delay otherwise? Tors could be clumsy, even stupid at times. The com port looked fine though. He rechecked his incoming dispatches. Still nothing.

Steffen was about to dispatch Tors when a flurry of activity near the side gates of the Martian Hideaway caught his eye. It was that scruffy-looking man again. He was leaving the Martian Hideaway and this time he was not alone. Behind him was a woman carrying a child in a basket, and behind her, a little girl.

Steffen leaned forward to look, forgetting his annoyance at the Imperial dispatcher and Tors. That girl could have been Fia. Only Steffen knew she was not. Had Fia lived, she would have been fifteen now. But this was how he remembered her. Steffen adjusted his mechanical eye, fixing it to zoom in on the girl. The colors were different. Fia's curls were flaxen when this girl's were dark, and she did not have Fia's pink complexion either. But other than that, she could have been Fia frozen in time.

Steffen's com port buzzed, but he barely heard it. His longing eyes were glued on the girl who struggled to keep up with the rest of the group.

"Slow down." A guttural growl slipped out of Steffen. He wanted the scruffy man to pay attention. How were a child's tiny feet supposed to keep up with a grown man's rushed steps?

They stopped, as if hearing Steffen's order. The man turned and talked to the girl. Steffen adjusted his earpieces, hoping to catch a bit of the conversation . . . her voice. It did not come through — too many people and too much noise around. He could see her clearly enough though, and there was no doubt about who was in charge of that conversation. She stood, tiny arms crossed, muttering angrily at the man. Steffen smiled, remembering how Fia had taken him to task for forgetting his medicines. "I'm disappointed in you, Babi," was the last thing she had said to him.

Steffen could not stop the memories from barging in. Fia, lying in a pool of blood, lifeless. They had fired on the playground. It was an encounter between two units of the brutal smuggling outfit YS Brotherhood, the reports said. Twenty-eight children died. Among them, Fia.

Steffen had waited for Lissel. She would know how to cope, he'd thought. She'd help him find a reason to live. But when Lissel refused to come back to Ajokkan, not even to cremate Fia's battered remains, he knew life was over. The only reason Steffen kept on living was his need for revenge. He began to prepare, gathering information and resources. Being a clerk at the Imperial Intelligence Bureau, he knew people with connections to arms and ammunitions suppliers. It did not take long to gather what he needed.

Fifteen days later, he had walked into the den of the YS Brotherhood. He was armored to the max to make up for his absolute lack of combat experience. He had chalked out a solid scheme to break in, but had no plan to get out. Steffen was prepared to die; he was ready to kill. The Brotherhood did not expect an ordinary man to break into their HQ. Steffen did not expect to enjoy blowing people to pieces.

Steffen had woken up in a hospital bed, covered from head to foot in swaths of bandages. People in sharp uniforms — top bosses of the Intelligence Bureau — welcomed him back to life. They commended him for his bravery and invited him to join their covert Assassin Corps. He had skills, they'd said. He could help clean up the streets, they'd said. He could stop mindless massacres from happening again, they'd said.

He'd agreed.

He kept on living, forgetting what he was living for. Until he only lived to kill. He did not care who was good and who was bad, he did not care if the lines got blurred a little, and he did not even notice if the lines disappeared entirely. Steffen Pere became an assassin with a reputation unmatched.

The com port buzzed again. Steffen blinked to clear his blurred vision. The little girl was gone. The group had turned the corner and disappeared. Two deep breaths, and Steffen could think somewhat clearly once more. On his wrist, the com flashed frantically.

Steffen blinked once more. It was the visual confirmation he was waiting for, a picture of . . .

That little girl?

For long, uncomprehending moments, Steffen simply stared at those wide brown eyes on a dusky face.

They want me to kill a child?

That he could not do. Steffen Pere had crossed many lines and done a million things that could make the fiercest soldier shudder, but he was not about to do this. He was going to walk away. His first failure in years — that was what this mission would stay.

He looked up once more in the direction the group had disappeared with his target in tow. His eyes narrowed immediately as questions bombarded his mind.

Who was that man in black with a stealthy gait? He could not be the child's father. Could he be another assassin they'd sent to take her out?

No!

Steffen scrambled out of the furrow and felt his legs for the walk assist. He needed speed to help that girl. If he wasn't too late already.

CLASH

Mako Nuyin

All Mako wanted to do was take Noell and her children someplace safe. He considered taking them home. His father would not mind if they stayed there for a day or two. After that, he could find a better place.

Weimen and Bea protested their leaving, but Noell did not listen. "I can't have people getting hurt because of us. I need to go where Luca won't find us. Perhaps going with Mako is the best way to dodge him. He won't imagine I would leave with a stranger."

She was right. The only way to deceive an enemy was to do something he'd expect the least. The element of surprise was a mighty weapon; they taught it early during Special Ops training. That a battered wife from a burned-out planet would propose it was unexpected. Perhaps a code for survival — an instinct — was ingrained in the genes.

Mako calculated his route back home. It would not take too long if he found a streetcar fast enough. He led Noell and her children out of the Martian Hideaway and toward the end of the street, where the streetcars had a pickup center. They had to get out of there quickly. Who knew what the crazy husband had found out from Arum? Maybe he knew his wife was at the Martian Hideaway. Mako strode faster.

"Stop!" a little voice shouted. Mako turned to face a pouting Eos. She tried to cross her tiny arms while glaring angrily at Mako. "You have to go slow," she chided. "Mama's carrying Jovan, can't you see? She can't run like you."

Mako looked at her puckered face and then at the dimming skies, almost thinking of telling her that he was running for her own good.

"I'm sorry," he said instead. "Should've thought of that. My mistake. Please forgive me."

Seeing her face soften, Mako turned toward Noell, who was still trying to catch her breath. "I can carry the baby if you'd like," he offered. "But we need to hurry. We have to reach the streetcars quickly. It's just two nodes away."

A few moments later, they were rushing again, now Mako carrying the infant in his basket. One more turn and they would only be steps away from the pickup center. Mako stiffened the moment they turned. There was a line of streetcars in the distance, but the stretch of road that lay in between was unexpectedly quiet. The back entrances of eateries lined it, their dark and shade screamed a perfect backdrop for illicit activity. His steps slowed by instinct, but the sight of the streetcars in the distance made him fight the anxiety away.

I'm worrying needlessly, Mako told himself.

He picked up the pace again.

He had taken no more than ten steps when Mako realized his blunder. Shadows fell across their path, and then three men blocked their way completely.

Someone gasped and broke into a sob behind him. Noell, he recognized. Mako set the child's basket on the ground and reached for his Pontuvin as the three men approached. The man in the middle was . . . Mako stiffened, recognizing that rugged, handsome face. His fingers curled firmly around the cold grip of his Pontuvin.

It was, without a doubt, Eos's father, Luca.

There was a rush of movement behind him—Noell ran to grab the basket Mako had set down. Eos clung to her mother, peeping at Luca from behind her, her usually luminous eyes now clouded with fear.

"That your wife Noell?" one of the two burly men clad in short tunics typical of northern Houndsmen asked the tall man who was standing in the middle.

The man in the middle—Luca, the dreaded husband—stepped forward.

"She's pretty," said the Houndsman, chuckling.

"Yes, thank you," Luca replied, running his fingers through longish hair that reached his shoulders.

"Told you the old man gave us the right location," the other Houndsman said. "You were worried about nothing."

Luca did not say a word. He moved closer, one step at a time, his eyes fixed on Mako's face.

"Please, sir." He addressed Mako in a soft, almost pleading voice. "This is a family matter. All I want is to speak to my dearest wife." He looked at Noell, his eyes barely betraying any emotion.

"No!" Noell said between sobs, "I don't want to."

"You hurt Uncle Arum," Eos's little voice accused.

Mako saw a hint of impatience pass over Luca's face, but it faded almost instantly.

"Oh no, dear god, no," he said, casting a beseeching look at Noell and Eos. "I could never . . . It was these bums. They — "

"No, you're lying!" Noell wailed.

"Ask them," Luca implored. He turned to Mako, his eyes glistening. "She's angry with me. We had a big fight and I admit, I behaved . . . horridly. But did she have to leave me like this? Believe me, I'd never hurt Arum or anyone else. I love my family."

His voice broke, and in that moment, Mako felt a little sorry for the man. Maybe he had made a mistake, but he seemed to regret it now. Mako had known a few flighty women himself. They knew how to make a mess of things over petty matters.

"My family is all I have," Luca continued in a broken voice. "I came here, like a madman, looking for my wife and my children. I love my wife. Everything I do, I do for her. Ask my wife. Who gets the best jewels on Robben-Xiu for her? Tell him, Noell."

He turned to Noell, and she flinched.

Mako did not know what to think. This man — a man who could have his pick of girls on Robben-Xiu given his obvious wealth — had crossed the galaxy looking for his lost family. That had to amount to something.

"Go on," Luca pleaded again. "Ask my wife. Ask Noell. Ask if I love her."

Mako turned to look at Noell. She was cowering, Eos clinging to her leg. Mako saw their eyes widen, but their scream was lost in the pain that erupted on the side of his face. Mako went flying for an endless moment until he hit the dusty road with a bone-rattling thud. The Pontuvin fell from his hand and clinked away. From the corner of his eye he saw Luca flex his fist, heard the Houndsmen chuckle, and tasted blood. Darkness poured over him.

***

Sounds trickled in. Sobs, threats, choked voices, pleas. Mako did not know where he was, until he remembered. Luca—Eos's father and Noell's husband—had hit him.

"You thought you could run away from me, Noell?" Luca snarled. Mako tried to turn his head, but he could not. His head felt too heavy, almost like a stone connected to his shoulders.

"After all I paid to get you, you think I'd let you wander away as you please?"

"Let her go!" Eos screamed.

"Shut up or I'll kill you. Kill all of you."

Mako opened his mouth to protest, but no sound came out. Shadows towered over him. Those Houndsmen—Luca's helpers. One of them grabbed Mako by the throat.

"Kill him?" the man asked, squeezing his throat.

"What else?" the other man replied.

Hands tightened around his neck. Air, he needed air. Darkness was closing in once more when Mako heard the tinkling noise. It was an odd, unnatural sound, sweeping toward them in a mad, frenzied rush. Then the lights faded once more.

RELEASE

Steffen Pere

The shriek that pierced the darkening skies made a cavernous hole in Steffen's guts. Cursing under his breath, he set the walk-assist—tiny motors built into his knees—to maximum and ran. He went clinking across the paved road, streaking past the walls encircling the Martian Hideaway, around the bend, and toward the distant huddle of people. Steffen was thoroughly disappointed in himself, but he did not let the frustration slow him down. Urgency to save the little girl before that man from the Special Ops struck her down coursed through him and set his senses on fire.

He pulled out his laserglaive when he was ten steps away. As he approached, mechanical eye adjusting rapidly to the dim light, the huddle loosened. They had all heard him, and now they turned to look.

The organizer in Steffen's brain unfurled as soon as he saw the man lying on the ground. The scruffy man, whom he suspected was from the Special Ops, the one he thought was sent to eliminate the girl, was lying on the ground, blood trickling out of his mouth. He was conscious, but barely.

Two burly men hovering over the fallen man snarled at Steffen as he drew closer.

Who are these men? Are they trying to help the girl?

A groan, the sound of someone choking, drifted to his ears. Steffen looked past the two men to the third, who was standing beyond. This man was good-looking and tall. He was somehow different from the tunic-clad duo hunched over the man on the ground. But why was he holding the young woman by her throat? The girl, doubtless her daughter, was pulling the man's other arm, frantic. The man paid no attention. Held in his grip, the woman

- 157 -

gasped for air.

It barely took Steffen the fraction of a second longer to comprehend the situation. He spent another fraction pulling out his Repsatz shredder knife. Steffen reached the two thugs before they could step forward. He caught them half-crouched, preparing to lunge at him.

"Hey!" one of them yelled. "Stay away. This is none of your busine—"

The laserglaive was buried to the hilt in the man's chest before he could get all his words out. Steffen did not hesitate to push the Repsatz into the other man's belly. Even before the second man erupted in a shower of blood globules, Steffen addressed the third man holding the woman.

"Let her go," he hissed.

The man stepped away in an instant and held his arms up.

"There, she's free," he said, flashing a lopsided smile. "But this is my family. You're intruding."

"Am I?"

"Yes," he shouted, pointing at the Special Ops man on the ground. "That man ... he tried to hurt my family. He and his ... people. Thank you for saving us. Tell him, Noell. Tell him."

The woman clasped her neck and kept on sobbing. Not a word escaped her lips, and she did not even look up.

"She's just scared," the man said. "My Noell gets scared easily. I need to just talk to her. Please—"

"No, he lies." The little girl's voice tinkled through the stale evening air that reeked of blood. Her words had the hint of a lisp, yet it was like a bell ringing on a mountaintop—clear and striking. "Mako was helping us. But he," she said, pointing an accusing finger at the tall man with long hair, "my papa was hurting Mama. He always hurts Mama."

"Eos, stop. She's just a child," the man said, chuckling nervously. "She doesn't know what she's—"

"I do!" Eos snapped. "You're a bad man. That's why we ran away from you. We hate you."

"You lying, ungrateful mutt." Words trickled out of the man's mouth like slow-flowing poison. "I should've killed you that night. I should've—" He stopped abruptly, remembering Steffen. He let out a laugh, his cheek dimpling slightly. "My daughter's difficult to handle sometimes. But I love her anyway. She's . . . they're all I've got. My family."

The air was too warm for comfort. Steffen suddenly felt the weight of every piece of metal they had put in him. Anger coiled like a snake inside his gut and left a trail of fire around the edges of his skull.

This man was a father. But instead of protecting his child with his life, he wished to kill her. Fate was peculiar.

Steffen wanted to crush every bone in the man's body, rip those perfect teeth out of his mouth one by one. He stepped forward, and with every step he took, the man fell back. Until he hit a wall.

"You don't know the first thing about family," Steffen said when he was close enough to look into the man's eyes. "You're the vilest thing I've set my eyes on."

Steffen saw the light fade from the man's face. His jaw tightened and his eyes flashed.

"They're *mine*," the man said, releasing the words slowly as if he were not ready to let them go. "I'll do whatever I want to do with them. They belong to me. And you can do nothing to change that, you sewn-up corpse of—"

Steffen simply meant to slap him, but his metal elbow happened to crash into the man's face, sending him tumbling to the ground. Steffen's fingers curled around his laserglaive, but he hesitated. He could do that later, when the family was gone. For now a restraint would be enough. He slipped a hoop snare over the man's neck and walked over to the man the girl called "Mako."

"Get up," Steffen ordered, tapping Mako's shoulder. It took a few more taps and spraying a mist of nerve stimulant on his face before Mako opened a bleary eye. He blinked a few times before frowning.

"Who are you?" Mako croaked, heaving as he tried to stand up straight.

"You don't need to know," Steffen replied.

The way Mako looked at him, eyeing his metal implants, it was obvious that he knew already.

"You must be —"

"I said, you do not need to know," Steffen reiterated, fixing a stare on Mako's pain-dulled eyes. He pointed at Eos and her family. "Do you intend to keep them safe?"

Mako did not hesitate. "Of course," he said. "I'll take them to a safe place."

"You should take them far away from here, you understand?"

Mako nodded.

"There are people who are out to harm —"

"I know," Mako interrupted. "They're trying to kill the girl."

Steffen froze. *How does he know that?*

"They had sent me after her." Mako seemed eager to explain. "It's something to do with the Eternity Prophecy. They've killed an oracle to suppress the real prophecy. But you know that, don't you?"

Steffen stared at Mako. This man knew Steffen had killed the oracle. How he knew that Steffen could not fathom, but he had to admit — this man, Mako, had guts to call him out.

"Why are you helping the girl?" Mako asked.

"You do not need to know. Make me say that one more time and you won't live to see another day."

Mako looked away, jaws tightening. Steffen could tell he was more annoyed than fearful but it was an apt and necessary end to Mako's probing. Steffen decided to veer the conversation away.

"If any harm comes to them . . . to her, I promise you I'll —"

"You have my word. I'll keep them safe," Mako interrupted again. Steffen did not like interruptions. Any other time, he would've been offended enough to kill, but something in Mako's eyes made him relent. He saw guilt. That was probably because he had failed to protect this family once. He also saw honesty. Mako seemed dependable.

Steffen let go of Mako's arm and glanced at the family huddled in the shadows. The woman was on her knees, whimpering still, her arms tight around her children. From the shelter of her mother's arms, the little girl stared intently at Steffen, making him bristle.

She has to be thinking of my weirdness, Steffen thought, pulling the cowl low over his metal-encrusted head.

"What will you do with Luca?" Mako nodded at the unconscious man caught in Steffen's snare.

Steffen looked Mako in the eyes and parted his lips. That was the closest he could get to smiling. "I'll spend some time with him. After that, he'll be free."

Mako's eyes narrowed. Perhaps he understood what Steffen meant to do with Luca, perhaps not. Steffen did not care. He only hoped Mako would not poke further.

"You should leave now," Steffen said.

"Yes," Mako replied simply.

Steffen watched as they shuffled their way to the line of streetcars in the distance. They had not taken twenty steps when they stopped. The little girl broke away from the huddle and ran toward him.

No one looked at Steffen's face anymore. He did not let them. He knew revulsion and fear would darken their eyes when they glimpsed his battered face. It was an ugly lump of deep gashes, some stitched, and some filled with metal. His good eye was sunk deep under a swollen bulge of an eyelid, the other embedded with telescoping gear. He was hideous, and he knew that all too well.

But when Eos ran toward Steffen, he did not know what to do. An assassin of the highest caliber, Steffen prided himself on his quick thinking, but he was not prepared for this. Then he panicked.

What is she going to do? Look at me up close? She'll get nightmares for years.

He tugged at the hood and lowered it farther over his face.

A few steps away from Steffen, she slowed. But she did not stop until she was right in front of him. Tilting her tear-streaked face up at him, she smiled. Steffen could not feel her fingers curling around his metal appendages; he only saw Fia standing in front of him. He fell on his knees and looked into her eyes, seeing in her the daughter he had lost, not even realizing that Eos had thrown her arms around his neck.

"Thank you," she whispered into his mangled ears. Her puny arms squeezed his neck one more time and then, just as suddenly as she had run to him, she ran away.

Around Steffen, the world blurred.

EXPOSE

Bryanna Tu-Fei

Bryanna's fingers hung above the portal's command catalog, as if frozen. From time to time they trembled, ever so slightly. She had let her fingers hover for a while, not knowing whether to let them plunge on the "Confirm" button.

Bryanna had worked all night putting things in place. First, she had completed her daily tasks. Then, with extreme care, she had extracted the contents of the tiny data store Lillyan and Satyak had given her. She had studied the layout of the data pipelines Cognitivus owned until she knew the location of every major hub and intersection in the network spanning the Empire. One by one, she had accessed the hubs and placed a capsule of compressed data — Lillyan and Satyak's brilliant handiwork — and the attached trigger inside them.

Those hubs were all she needed. Even if she could not get to the ones farther away from her spatially, as in those in the next planetary system, as long as she got to every hub in Ajokkan she'd be in good stead. Her plan: place a capsule in every intersection along with a trigger. As soon as incoming data came across a hub, the trigger inside it would be activated and transmit the capsule of information to the portal that had sent the incoming data. Within moments, the networks crisscrossing Ajokkan would be swamped by twice the traffic it was expected to handle. Maybe some of the hubs would crash. Bryanna cringed at the thought — that would add another offense to her list. She chided herself immediately for the momentary surge of fear. What needed to be done had to be done quickly.

Bryanna knew she was running out of time. Outside the large glass windows of the Cognitivus building, the sky was turning a delicate shade of purple. Soon her shift would end and she'd have to leave. She'd have to wait until the following night before she could get another chance to reveal that Magetha had tampered with a prophecy. Bryanna doubted if they'd let her live that long.

The truth had to come out *now*.

The truth? What if I'm simply imagining things? Bryanna pulled her hovering arm away.

It was possible. Maybe the yellow-haired guard who she thought was spying on her simply lived near her house. Maybe he had recognized her as a neighbor when she was leaving Cognitivus. That would explain his presence at the café next door yesterday.

But no, it did not explain his being there at the café *all day*. No one spent an entire day at an eatery, unless they had a reason to be there.

Perhaps he was sweet on a waitress.

No, that did not explain his staring at her windows. He *had* to be watching her. Someone had sent him after her, and it could not be Cognitivus. If Cognitivus were after her, wouldn't they restrict her from coming to her shift? It had to be someone else; it *had* to be Magetha and the Order of Divine Sight.

Once again, in a slow, hesitant creep, Bryanna's hand drew closer to the "Confirm" button.

Bryanna wished *she* could predict the future. She wished she could see the effect of pressing that button. This action, like every other action, would have repercussions. Only this one would change her life in an instant. She did not know if it would be for the better or the worse, but she would certainly cease to be the woman she was now. She could be called a criminal and thrown into the Empire's deepest dungeon, or she could be hailed a hero. Bryanna wished she knew which it would be.

One thing she knew for sure — the Data Sanctity Enforcement Unit, the DASEU, would arrest her. If she were lucky enough, she'd make it out of the building, but she would not make it home. They'd probably be here before she crossed the next street. Yes, that was how long it would take the DASEU to jump-start the constabularies into action.

They would send a hundred patrols after her as soon as they detected the source of the disruption. Bryanna deserved their attention too. Yes, the kind of snare she had laid out in the Cognitivus pipelines would cause instant pandemonium. Every user of the networks would be affected like they had never been before. The DASEU would know of the disruption right away.

They would dive in with everything they had to find the culprit. It would not take them long to trace it to the Cognitivus building and to Bryanna's portal. Not because she was not smart enough to cover her tracks, but because she did not have any reason to hide them from the DASEU. She did not *care* if the DASEU flagged her as a criminal and sent the constabularies to arrest her for planting the disruptive trigger in the Cognitivus networks. All she wanted was to let people know of the ODS's crime.

Bryanna thought over the sequence of attack one last time, checking for possible inconsistencies. It was a clear handshake protocol—the sender of any information into the networks of Cognitivus would receive something back today, courtesy of Bryanna and the capsule she had planted in the networks. Since all electronic transactions in the Empire was conducted through the Cognitivus pipelines, it meant every citizen would possibly receive Bryanna's note. Only it would not be a pleasant greeting, but an ominous one Bryanna had laboriously penned during the day.

Hello, honorable subject of the glorious Veloressian Empire!

If you are seeing this, I have succeeded. I may be dead but my death has not been in vain, for I have your eyes, your ears, and your attention. I know you will carry on my fight even when I am gone, for this fight is yours just as much as it is mine.

Why should I fight, you ask? Because the holiest of holies, the cornerstone of our faith, the most sacred of all prophecies — the Eternity Prophecy — has been violated.

The Order of Divine Sight and its leaders, the ones we endowed with the powers to protect our most sacred beliefs are the ones who have destroyed it. Why, I do not know. That is for you to find out.

I send you all I have, the irrefutable proof of the crime that has been committed against our Gods, our beliefs, and the Empire.

Blessed seeing!

The evidence she had gathered in the last few days would follow, the proof of the crime — tampering with Prophecy Archives records — the Order of Divine Sight had committed, all of which Lillyan and Satyak had compressed into the tiny capsule.

"All right, then," Bryanna whispered. Kianto's happy face flashed in front of her eyes, the memory stretching her lips into a satisfied smile. She was going to avenge his death after all. She looked around — her shoulder-sack was packed and ready, the data store plugged into the portal's receptacle. Drawing a full, deep breath, Bryanna tapped "Confirm."

"It's done," she whispered, partly in relief and partly out of fear of what was coming. She watched as the command replicated itself and sped across the network, stopping at each hub to arm the trigger. One by one, the hubs lit up. Soon, the automonitors would detect the abnormal traffic. And then . . .

Bryanna picked up her shoulder-sack and trudged toward the elevator. She had to get out of there before the alarms started blaring.

***

Bryanna did not harbor any hopes of reaching home. With the shape her hips were in, she knew she'd be lucky to reach the next street. If there could be miracles, she'd wish to visit Nico and the rest of the brood one last time.

Bryanna cast a quick look around as she exited the building. A regular morning crowd — people rushing to get to work — thronged the walkways. All was still well in Ajokkan. But not for long, Bryanna mused. Smiling to herself, she hobbled in the direction of the pet sanctuary, weaving past distracted pedestrians. She had almost reached the nearest street node when the back of her neck prickled. Something was . . . not normal.

Is someone watching me? Following me?

Bryanna's grip on her shoulder-sack tightened. She stopped and looked around, eyes scanning the crowds. It had to be *him*. That fake guard, the yellow-haired man in brown overalls who'd been tailing her was somewhere close, Bryanna was sure. But hard as she tried, she couldn't spot him.

"Can't just stand here like a fool," Bryanna muttered after a while. She had to keep going. Bracing herself, she stepped forward, the sound of sirens hitting her ears almost immediately. Bryanna slowed. It was the unmistakable clanging of constabulary vehicles drawing near. They zipped past her, their bodies flashing yellow, and impinged on the front doors of the Cognitivus.

Bryanna kept walking, her head low, eyes scanning the pavement. She stood on one side of the crowd forming at the crossing. It was a pedestrian blockage, the cycle during which the street closed to pedestrians. Bryanna was counting down impatiently to the end of the blocking time when she noticed the yellow blob drawing close.

It was him — the man with yellow hair, the one who had been stalking her.

He was rushing in her direction, eyes skimming the road, his hands tucked inside the pockets of his overalls. He was almost hurtling toward her, unseeing. Bryanna cast a frantic look around. She was standing at the edge of the road, streetcars and larger transports whizzing past without a care.

Why isn't he slowing down?

The way he was dashing, he would bump into the crowd and knock someone into the traffic.

It took her a long, petrified moment to realize what was

happening. He was coming to get her. He was planning to push *her* into the road. He was about to kill her.

Perhaps she was wrong, perhaps she was too nervous to think straight, but Bryanna did not want to take her chances on the questionable man.

As fast as her legs could carry her ungainly body, she stepped away and walked in the only direction she could — back toward the entrance of the Cognitivus. The man with yellow hair stumbled to a halt. He looked up, and, as his gaze met Bryanna's, she knew her suspicions were true. Frustration rippled across his pale face; his eyes flashed. For a moment both of them stood still, measuring each other up. Then he dashed toward her once more.

Bryanna did not miss the way the bottoms of his pockets bulged.

He has to have weapons in there.

Ignoring the dryness of desert sands spreading through her throat, Bryanna hobbled toward the front door of the Cognitivus, which was now lit a vivid yellow by the gathered vehicles. Agents of the constabularies, all clad in black and armored like fortresses, patrolled the area. She only had to get near them. Behind her, almost within arm's distance, the yellow-haired man followed. He was too close. Another step and he would reach her. And if he reached her, whatever weapon he had hidden would kill her. Bryanna did not want to die. Not now. Not yet. She was open to a martyr's death, but only after someone had heard her story. An inglorious death on the pavement was not acceptable.

With all her might, Bryanna screamed, "No, I won't let you! Go away!"

The agents turned to look. A good look, and they would recognize her as the woman in their warrant.

"Go away!" she shouted again. She knew, behind her, the stalker had stopped.

Drawing his weapon, one agent stepped forward. Then another. Then one more.

"It's her!" someone yelled. They had recognized her.

"Don't move!" the agent in front shouted.

Bryanna knew they would pay no attention to the yellow-haired man. Her would-be assassin would flee. She was not going to let that happen. Bryanna fell back an unstable step or two and grabbed the yellow-haired man's overalls.

"Don't hurt him!" she shrieked as the agents closed in around them. The yellow-haired man tried to loosen her grip, tugging, pushing to break free.

"Don't move!" the agents shouted again. "Hold your arms out."

"Please let him go. It wasn't his fault. He didn't know what he was doing," Bryanna wailed, fingers clutching the man's overalls tighter. "I planned it all. He was only a helper."

Booted feet thundered toward them. A cloud of black gathered around her, forming an impenetrable wall. Strong arms grabbed her and pulled her away.

They put her in one of the largest vehicles. As it sped away, Bryanna saw them force the yellow-haired man into another. Chuckling loudly, she leaned back and closed her eyes.

She got him after all. She got them all.

4

Chaos begets order, order begets contentment, and contentment begets degeneration.

—Adi Niappan of the water world

CATHARSIS

Two days after the scandal broke, Sister Subordinate Xihin waited alone at the Hall of Sightings. All around her, the stiff backs of empty chairs glistened and shone. Her oracles were still at the final round of questioning; Xihin knew she had to wait for a while before anyone arrived.

Two tedious and shameful days had passed since every constabulary in Ajokkan had unleashed their forces on the foundation buildings. They had escorted Sister Paramount Magetha out first, and then held every resident of the Order in the isolation of their rooms. They had wanted to stop the residents from speaking to one another. They could not stop the mentanets though. By the time they took Oracle Junior Ainer Ahloi away, murmurs of the biggest scandal in centuries reverberated throughout the hallowed buildings of the Order of Divine Sight.

On the second day of the siege, Xihin was called into interrogation. She told them everything she knew: the missing Oracle Prime Leon Courtee, the note Leon left in her office, and Magetha's subtle warning when she'd asked about Leon. They told her how Magetha had confessed to Leon's murder.

Xihin could barely think straight when they let her go. She had known Magetha for a while, worshipped her for long, and she could not have imagined for one moment that Magetha could be capable of ordering a man—one of her own oracles—murdered. They of the oracle clusters were supposed to be facilitators of the Gods in ruling the Empire. When had they turned into soulless demons?

When the interim chair of the Order called Xihin and asked her help in keeping the foresight sessions running while the Order endured the probe, Xihin jumped at the chance. She was undoubtedly shaken by the scandal, but her faith in the ODS and the Veloressian prophecy system was still firm. She had dreamed of being part of the oracle clusters since she was a child, and being the supervisor of the oracles at ODS had been a long and fulfilling journey. She'd do anything to keep the Order going.

That morning they told her something new. The investigators had recovered a part of Oracle Prime Courtee's erased prophecy. It mentioned a girl. Just like Leon had said in his note to her. A girl — the first in thousands of years — was unexpected, unreal. As if fate had not laughed at them enough, it had to toss them this awakening call. "Open your minds," it seemed to say. "You're visionaries; you're supposed to see more than an ordinary Veloressian." They had closed their eyes, forgotten to look beyond the usual and the expected, and lost their way. She had to bring them back.

Since the morning, Xihin had waited at the Hall of Sightings. Her oracles trickled in, shoulders sagging with collective guilt, their faces dim and downcast. When they had all assembled, she took the podium.

"Our order has failed," she started, wielding her sharp voice like a whip. "Unwittingly, we have become part of history. Ours is not a glorious part like we had hoped, but the darkest blemish. We should never forget this time."

Sighs rose. Bowed heads drooped even more.

"But we cannot give up either. Not just because we have faith in the prophecy system, but because we cannot let Oracle Prime Leon Courtee's vision die with him. He had seen the real Eternity Prophecy, but it was snatched away from him and discarded. We have to resurrect it. We owe it to the Veloressian Empire to bring their lost Holy One back to them."

Her oracles — every one of them — sat up, faces taut and eyes alert.

"Oracle Prime Leon Courtee, our own Leon, saw a girl whom Sister Paramount Magetha chose to throw away. We have to find her and bring her to the people of Veloressia. So I call upon you to see like you've never seen before. Let us find the Holy One the Veloressian Empire has lost."

BREATHE

Noell Rivans

This world was a fantastic shade of blue. Never in her life had Noell seen so much water. It was everywhere. A planet full of unending and wild water—imagine that. What the people of Robben-Xiu would give to have a tenth of it. They called the planet Ro'yen Att, meaning "Water World" in native Attrian tongue.

"Mama, Mama," Eos called, tugging Noell's sleeve. "How far down do we have to go?"

Noell knew precious little about Ro'yen Att. After arriving at the star base on this planet, Mako Nuyin had walked them over to giant elevators that carried people into the depths of the unending oceans covering the planet. They had boarded one and, for a long while after that, they had been sinking deeper and deeper into the blue.

"How far, Mama?"

Noell looked at Mako. He was hunched over the device on his wrist, punching its screen furiously with his fingers every now and then. He was communicating with someone, Noell figured. It would be rude to interrupt.

"Some more, I guess," Noell told Eos, pulling her closer. "Are you feeling all right?"

Eos nodded. "Yes. Wish Uncle Arum could be here."

Noell suppressed a sigh. Uncle Arum . . . he had risked his life for her when her own parents did nothing to protect her. If wishes could all come true, she would wish to be by his side now, help him when he needed it most. But that was not to be.

"We'll visit him someday. I promise." Noell patted Eos's head gently, until she felt her little body relax into a doze.

Outside, the blue grew deeper.

Is this it? The place where I will find a safe life for my children?

She stole another glance at Mako Nuyin, her gaze lingering over the side of his face that had turned purple from Luca's blow. Mako was a stranger, but he seemed trustworthy. He was helping them simply because Arum was his friend. He had found them a berth on the ship to Ro'yen Att. She could have never done that on her own. Mako's kindness was unexpected, almost too hard to believe.

Noell leaned back and closed her eyes, relishing the wave of relief that rippled through her muscles, calming and easing them. Yet, she still did not understand a lot of things.

Who was that man with metal implants? What did he want with them? And what happened to Luca?

It did not matter. As long as she was away from Luca, nothing else mattered. Noell did not know what the future held for them, but she was sure it would be better than it had been so far. She breathed in the strange air of the water world, enjoying the damp tingle of it in her nostrils, memorizing the faint smell of moisture. For the first time in years, Noell breathed without fear.

SINK

Mako Nuyin

For a long time, Mako could not decide if he should tell Noell. Then he did not know *what* to tell her. The more he thought about it, the more he hesitated. How would she react if she knew the truth about her daughter? And the truth about him? That he had followed them around not because Arum asked him to, but because he needed answers. That he had no good intentions for them to begin with. Extraction missions assigned to operatives like him were never meant to be friendly; they always ended in imprisonment or death for the target. If Eos had been his target, that did not exactly make him their friend.

But he felt he had to tell Noell about Eos, for her own sake and her children's. Then there was this new thing Kerl had dispatched him about—the breaking news that the Eternity Prophecy was falsified. Just like Leon had told Roli. Now that the truth was out, the oracles would start looking for the next Adi Niappan again, and they would eventually find out about Eos.

Eos's mother *had* to know.

The elevator was halfway down to settlement level when Mako decided to come clean. The woman was staring out the curved windows of the capsule, her gaze calm. The infant slept peacefully in her lap, and Eos, her head resting on her mother's arm, seemed fast asleep as well. They were at peace.

It'd be a sin to shatter that. It'd also be a sin to keep lying.

"Sorry," Mako started casually, edging closer to Noell. "Is everything all right with the . . . children?"

Noell turned, her eyes widening for a moment. She nodded slowly.

"Your face . . ." Her voice trailed off.

Mako touched the side of his face, twitching. It was swollen, and it hurt like hell. That Luca was strong.

"It'll be fine in a day or two."

"Thank you," she said. "Thank you for helping us. And for getting us here."

"Thought it'd be good to take you away from Ajokkan and Planet Central."

She did not reply. Her thoughtful gaze quietly scanned his face. It was a torture to be scrutinized like that. Or maybe she was not scrutinizing at all. Maybe it was just his conscience that screamed for release.

"It's a mess in Ajokkan today," he said, breaking the stifling silence. "There's a big scandal about the Eternity Prophecy."

Her deep amber eyes locked on his, questioning. Yet not a word escaped her lips. She was a quiet one, the kind he was not used to.

"They found out the last Eternity Prophecy was false. No one saw the Adi Niappan in a boy from New Haphniss."

Noell gasped, as was expected. Faking any prophecy was unthinkable, but faking the Eternity Prophecy? Even Mako did not have a word to describe that.

"Why, then . . ."

"Nothing's clear yet. There's a lot of speculation. Some are saying they needed an excuse to wage war on New Haphniss, so . . ."

"How did they find out?"

"Apparently a woman discovered the fraud and broadcasted proof of it to every citizen in the Empire," Mako said.

If faking the Eternity Prophecy was unbelievable, then a middle-aged, commonplace woman uncovering the conspiracy was just as unreal. Kerl said the masses, smitten by the woman's courage and brilliance, were calling her the Prophet of Truth. Per Kerl's dispatch, massive processions — the likes of which he had never seen before — had taken over Ajokkan, demanding the woman's immediate release from the constabulary holding her.

Noell's amber eyes had grown a shade darker. "What kind of proof?" she asked, her voice barely a whisper.

"This morning she hacked into the Cognitivus pipelines. She hid a trigger in the pipelines somehow. Every time a transaction came through, a message was sent to the originator. It contained proof that the chief of the Order of Divine Sight erased a prophecy at the archives. By midmorning, half of Ajokkan had the proof of fakery in their hands."

Noell inhaled sharply and held it. Even before Mako looked up at her, he knew her face would be drained of color. This was a crime unheard of: in the Veloressian Empire, information was sacred, and the Prophecy Archives were considered holier than holy. Deleting a record from there was sacrilege.

"And isn't that the same order that—"

"Claimed the Eternity Prophecy, yes," Mako completed for her.

"Why did they erase a prophecy?"

"The theory is that they deleted the real Eternity Prophecy so they could put the fake one about the boy into the archives."

Noell shook her head and turned away. She kept shaking her head from time to time until she turned to Mako again.

"Where did you hear all this?"

"Kerl dispatched me. Didn't get it until now since I was off the grid."

"Who's Kerl?"

"He's my . . . friend."

"Oh." On Noell's lap, the baby stirred. She shifted a little to make him comfortable.

"So . . . if the Adi Niappan is not on New Haphniss like they announced, then where is he?"

Mako wanted to tell her everything—about Eos, about how Noell's daughter was the next Holy One, about Leon's vision, about how the same people who had faked the Eternity Prophecy had plotted to kill her daughter, about how they had sent not just the cybernetic assassin but also Mako's team to eliminate the child. Yet he could not make himself do it.

It was her face that stopped him. Her face was free of pain and of fear, and not rigid with anticipation. It was clean, like a sheet of glass washed by the rain.

She did not need to know anything yet. For now he could guard their secret.

"No one knows," Mako lied.

There was no war in New Haphniss that needed him anyway. He could stay in Ro'yen Att for now. He could watch over Eos and her family for a while.

RESURRECTION

The Teesar Nettara was not an oracle cluster of high standing. In fact, in the hierarchy of the Veloressian prophecy system it did not have much standing at all.

Located in the shoddy northern outskirts of the Empire's capital Ajokkan, the Nettarians — as the monks and oracles of that order were commonly known — made it a point to not think too highly of themselves. Even though they often came in touch with the more famed clusters in Ajokkan, particularly the leading ten, the Nettarian monks knew their rather tiny cluster composed of only nineteen oracles was nothing compared to their larger and more famous peers.

The Nettarians operated quietly and humbly. Their oracles were neither ambitious nor gifted enough to try visualizing the Adi Niappan, but simply glorified fortune-tellers to the local population. They were content to remain that way, particularly after the scandal of the faked Eternity Prophecy shocked Ajokkan and the Empire.

The Teesar Nettara and its limited coffers barely made it through the upheaval after the conspiracy became known. When a web of collusion that stretched from the Order of Divine Sight all the way to the Imperial Council came to light, followed by several prominent arrests, waves of suspicion and public outcry rocked every oracle cluster, big and small. However, troubling days passed, albeit slowly, and two months after the incident, a semblance of regularity and a steady trickle of coinage had returned to the cluster.

The official beginning of winter was supposed to be yet another mediocre day in the life of Senior Oracle Ausin Eves of the Teesar Nettara. He walked into the divination chamber that morning hoping to accomplish only one thing — a glimpse into the future of his client, one Tora Barme, to find out if her soldier husband would survive his recent deployment to New Haphniss. That was the only task assigned to him that day, and Ausin hoped to retire early and enjoy the customary bonfire and accompanying feast to celebrate the beginning of the new season.

His plans went awry the moment he slipped into the chair and fixed his gaze on the wall of swirling colors in front of him. He had started the divination process just the way he had done for the last fifty-five years, just the way it always worked for him. But instead of slipping in the direction he wanted to go, in the direction of Tora Barme's husband and the heavily forested world of New Haphniss, Ausin was dragged into a world of blue, to a planet with nothing but water for as far as he could see.

In his vision, Ausin drifted, skimming along the endless oceans covering the unexpected planet, to the giant, glass-covered star port that read "North Entry, Ro'yen Att." Down the massive elevators he went, descending into the bowels of the ocean. He floated past the entryway of the settlement level and along the serpentine corridors of the underwater colonies, past people of all colors, shapes, and sizes.

Until he faced a little girl.

Even in his vision, Ausin held his breath. That incandescent ring hovering above the tiny girl's head was something he had only read about in books and never expected to see. It was the halo of divinity, the mark put on an Adi Niappan by the Gods. They said the halo revealed itself only to the truly gifted and the blessed — and Ausin did not consider himself either.

Yet he could not stop seeing it dance over the curly-haired, dusky-skinned girl with laughing brown eyes and a crescent-shaped mark across her forehead. The import of this vision was not lost on Ausin. This was *the* girl, the future Adi Niappan every respectable oracle in the Empire was seeking. Ausin's eyes clung greedily to the fiery ring that swirled above her for as long as he could. Then like all visions, this one too came to an end and Ausin receded — all the way back into his lumpy and cold, leather-backed divination chair.

Ausin could be many things, but he was not crazy. Yet, when he rushed out of the divination chamber that morning, eyes sparkling with a riotous glee, his compatriots arranging the bonfire at the center of the courtyard thought the old man had lost it. A young monk rushed forward, concerned. With the lingering effects of the prophecy scandal, times were tough and the Teesar Nettara could not afford to lose an oracle now.

"Ausin!" he called. "Is everything —"

"I've seen her!" Ausin screamed, his gaze fixed on the rapidly brightening skies.

Everyone in the courtyard stopped to listen. A few even stepped closer.

"I've seen the Adi Niappan!" Ausin shouted, raising his trembling arms up at the skies as if to beckon the Gods. "I've been blessed by the Eternity Prophecy," Ausin gushed, choking near the end. His timeworn eyes, wrinkled at the corners, spilled a barrage of tears over his gaunt cheeks.

As Ausin broke into sobs, Nettarians — oracles and monks alike — fell to their knees around him. They knew that through Ausin Eves, they had all been blessed. Teesar Nettara would never be the same again, and neither would the Empire.

Appendix - 1

THE RELIGIO-POLITICAL STRUCTURE OF
THE VELORESSIAN EMPIRE

From the account of Principal Scribe Ibn Karoujah, serving historian of the Empire of Veloressia, by appointment of His Divine Grace, the Adi Niappan of the six moons.

The Empire, the official name of which is the Empire of Veloressia, grew from the remnants of the Old Confederacy. Broken to pieces by the Twenty-Year Wars, the scattered dominions were brought together two thousand years later by the Bodiyan Sect and their visions.

The Old Confederacy was founded on the principles of democracy, in which citizens elected a council of leaders through a drawn-out and complicated voting process that often took years to complete. In that old system, there was no concept of state-backed religion. There was no sanction against any form of preaching either. People practiced their own religions, and an organized religion often spread locally within nearby planet clusters. It is important to note that, even within these planet clusters, organized religion never developed the frenzied and zealous following that was often seen in prior civilizations.

Also worth noting is the fact that the Twenty-Year Wars were caused by economic factors rather than lack of faith in the government of the Confederacy. After the wars, when the Confederacy was split into independent planetary domains, the remnants of the old government largely stayed in place. They continued to govern their usual way, only now over discrete regions.

The Bodiyan Sect had existed on Neu Terra since the galaxy had been settled. The art of divination was an integral part of their religious customs. Their oracles — the ones who made significant progress into divination — were an elite coterie within the sect. Neu

Terra's proximity to Rolophim, a gas giant with magnetic and radiation fields rivalling a star's, is said to contribute to the enhanced mental capacities of the sect's visionary oracles. Later studies have shown this as plausible. While Rolophim's strong atmospheric influence on Neu Terrans was not dangerous to the settlers' health, it could have induced changes in physiology.

For thousands of years, while the Old Confederacy flourished, the Bodiyan Sect continued their practices, overlooked to a large extent. Overlooked, that is, except by its own followers, who were intent on becoming visionaries themselves. They flocked from near and far. Since spending time on Neu Terra was deduced a prerequisite for powers of divination, citizens of the confederacy often travelled across the galaxy to Neu Terra to bask in the influencing fields of Rolophim.

The sect's powers of foresight would have gone unnoticed if the Twenty-Year Wars did not break out. It is said that Tolmonth the Fifth, the Bodiyan Sect's thirty-first leader, had predicted the war that eventually tore the Confederacy apart. He had also seen the fall of the Confederacy, among other things. After the demise of the Confederacy, the story of this prophecy spread across the galaxy and, a few hundred years later, the sect had grown in size from a few thousand to nearly a million strong. Now numerous, the oracles of the Bodiyan Sect scattered across the galaxy over the next few centuries, carrying with them their practices.

On the various planets, the oracles were often itinerant and preached the ways of the Bodiyan Sect to the population. Considering they preached on planets that had little prior exposure to the sect, and considering most planets already had their own independent flavor of quasiorganized religion, it was only due to the now-extinct confederacy's open-mindedness about religion that these traveling preachers met with little resistance. Curiously enough, they were embraced by the existing religious orders, many of which eagerly hosted the oracles — partly out of curiosity and partly out of benevolence.

Within a thousand years after the fall of the Confederacy, the oracles of the sect had become rooted in every planet that had been a part of it, and considered integral to the indigenous religious orders. It was also around this time that the oracles and their visions became an economic tool in the hands of these orders. Selling visions and foretelling became a thriving business, and as the faith in the prophecies grew, so did the strength and influence of the orders. Of all the orders that assimilated the Bodiyan oracles unto themselves, none grew faster than the ones on Planet Central and specifically the capital city, Ajokkan. They called themselves oracle clusters, and their coffers filled fast. Understandably, they took to spreading the importance of prophecies with passion.

The Veloressian theocracy was foretold by an oracle in one such cluster — the Order of Divine Sight in Ajokkan — run by the Sisterhood of Plana. He is also said to have prophesied the destruction of the planet Eilen-Ra in the Hosloman System by asteroid strike. The idea that the death of nearly a billion people on Eilen-Ra could have been avoided had the prophecies been used efficiently became everyday lore. It successfully ignited the common citizen's fascination with and fervor for the oracles.

Around this time, a string of calamities struck the planetarchies — dual famines on X-20-Liel System and a near-extinction event caused by the explosion of a super volcano on Acsesion Prime among them — which resulted in the deaths of billions. When the oracles of five clusters spoke of a blessed being that would arrive to lift the planetarchies out of their misery and protect them from future calamities, their prophecy invaded the hearts of even the staunchest nonbeliever. The one chosen by the Gods — the Adi Niappan — was to be born among the citizens of the Old Confederacy to rejoin the planetarchies into one empire, they also said. The planetarchies acceded without much ado.

The first Adi Niappan was found in the now-defunct planet of Veloressia, then a four-year-old boy in a city at the brink of ecological devastation. His arrival in Ajokkan is deemed the beginning of the Veloressian Empire that spanned twenty-three stars.

The Adi Niappan

The Adi Niappan is the head of Veloressian theocracy and traditionally has been responsible for the governing of the Empire. Chosen by visions of the oracle clusters, an Adi Niappan is sanctified by the Bodiyan Sect's highest order, the Priests of Neu Terra.

According to Bodiyan beliefs, the current Adi Niappan is an embodiment of the forces of nature that surround the universe. He is the one selected by the Gods to rule the Empire in their stead. Every Adi Niappan is blessed with special powers—some have the power of foresight, some have the ability to heal, and some have been able to grant other miracles.

Every Adi Niappan also receives a piece of the previous Adi Niappan's soul after he has passed. In that sense, a living Adi Niappan holds the essence of all Adi Niappans before him.

It is said that an Adi Niappan can choose to move from his current life to the next by freeing his soul from his body whenever he desires. Once he has chosen the time to depart the world, he requests that the Grand Niappans begin the search for his successor. The customary beginning of the Great Search begins with a ten-day mourning period for the departing Adi Niappan. The Grand Niappans and the Imperial Council then commence the Great Search across the galaxy for a child who was born a few years before the search.

It can take one to two years to identify an Adi Niappan; it was two years before the current, seven hundredth, Adi Niappan, was found.

The process of finding an Adi Niappan is centered around the Veloressian prophecy system, and the process follows an order penned by the Priests of Neu Terra:

1. Vision of the location: One of the oracles in any of the Empire's oracle clusters may have a vision of the location where the Adi Niappan is born.

2. Vision of the identifying marks: The oracle who has seen the location of the Adi Niappan or a different oracle will have a vision of identifying marks on the Adi Niappan.

3. Approach of the Imperial Council: The Imperial Council will arrive at the abode of the Adi Niappan and present him with a number of holy artifacts belonging to the Bodiyan Sect and the Adi Niappans who came before him. If the child correctly identifies certain artifacts in the order expected, the Imperial Council accepts him as the new Adi Niappan.

4. Presentation at Neu Terra: The next step in sanctifying the new Adi Niappan is performed by the priests of the Bodiyan Sect in Neu Terra. Once the child appears before them, the priests go to a holy mountain to pray to Rolophim. If, during their seven-day prayers, they receive blessings from the mighty planet, the child is declared the new Adi Niappan.

5. Departing of the Old Adi Niappan: Only after a new Adi Niappan is blessed at Neu Terra does the old Adi Niappan give up his mortal body. According to the Bodiyan Sect's beliefs, he passes on to a higher world.

After the Adi Niappan is sanctified, it is time to bring him to the palace in Ajokkan. A group consisting of the five servants, the Grand Niappans, the Imperial Council, and a selected division of the Imperial Forces collects the boy and they travel to Ajokkan. If the child is younger than five, his parents are allowed to come and stay with him until he reaches his fifth year. At the Niappan's palace, the boy is trained in Bodiyan constructs and slowly introduced into responsibilities of government. Usually, by the age of ten, a boy is ready to independently assume the role of supreme leader of the Empire.

The Imperial Government

The Adi Niappan is the absolute power in the Empire and, at least in theory, wields complete control of the land and its resources. He is also the supreme military commander of the Imperial Forces and head of the Imperial government. He relies on a bureaucracy of officials to manage his affairs.

He has a grand council of ten advisers — the Grand Niappans — who are also chosen through visions of oracles. Just like the Adi Niappan, these advisers are also chosen for life; a new Grand Niappan is picked only when an old one has passed.

In charge of the administration is the Imperial Council, who act as the Adi Niappan's representatives and coordinate planetary economics, the Imperial treasury, the military, the legal system, the health and transportation systems, the information networks, and the archives.

The control of the prophecy system is not with the Imperial Council, but placed in the hands of the Conclave Prime — a group of ten leading oracle clusters.

At the next level, the Empire is divided into as many as forty-nine planetary regions called the protectorates, each governed by a planetarch, who is accountable to the Imperial Council for his jurisdiction.

Much of the economy is decentralized and not strictly controlled. But for a monthly tariff — often considered a hefty and unfair sum, a value set proportional to the planet's income — there is not much interference in the planetarch's administrative processes or demands on the planet's economy from the Empire.

Appendix - 2

LIST OF PRINCIPAL CHARACTERS

Magetha – Head of the Order of Divine Sight (ODS)

Leon Courtee – Prime Oracle of the ODS, neighbor and friend of Orin and Mako

Xihin – Junior member of the sisterhood, ODS

Noell Rivans – Woman from Robben-Xiu, Luca's wife, mother of Eos and Jovan

Luca Daksson – Legume farmer from Robben-Xiu, Noell's husband, father of Eos and Jovan

Eos – Daughter of Noell and Luca

Jovan – Son of Noell and Luca

Mako Nuyin – Member of the Special Ops, Imperial Intelligence Bureau, Orin's son

Orin Nuyin – Former soldier in the Imperial Forces, Mako's father

Arum – Bartender in Ajokkan, Mako's friend, Noell's uncle

Roli – Homeless boy in Ajokkan

Bryanna Tu-Fei – Data Organizer at Cognitivus, Kianto's mother

Kianto – Apprentice at the ODS, Bryanna's son

Steffen Pere – Assassin of the Imperial Intelligence Bureau, Lissel's husband, Fia's father

Lissel – Soldier in the Imperial Forces, Steffen's wife, Fia's mother

Fia – Daughter of Lissel and Steffen

Weimen Callum – Owner of Martian Hideaway, Bea's husband, Arum's friend

Bea Callum – Owner of Martian Hideaway, Weimen's wife

Lillyan Kosnaguri – Bryanna's former student, Satyak's twin sister

Satyak Kosnaguri – Bryanna's former student, Lillyan's twin brother

Ausin Eves – Senior Oracle at the Teesar Nettara oracle cluster

Acknowledgements

No book is created in a void and The Eternity Prophecy is certainly no exception. This story has come to life with support from many, and I want to thank you all.

First, I'd like to thank everyone who nominated the book and campaigned for it and promoted it during the Kindle Scout run. I'm looking at you my friends, my mailing list subscribers, the folks at kboards.com, and my critique group.

Special thanks go to my friend, cheerleader, and critic extraordinaire, Diana. This book would not be the same without your honest and succinct evaluation.

Also, thank you, Allison, for editing advice that went far beyond the usual and helped make a Kindle Scout run possible for The Eternity Prophecy.

Last, but definitely not the least, my sincere thanks to my family for their encouragement and unending support, especially the littlest one who shows me every day how selfless and powerful love can be.

About the Author

S. G. Basu is an aspiring potentate of a galaxy or two. She plots and plans with wondrous machines, cybernetic robots, time travelers and telekinetic adventurers, some of whom escape into the pages of her books. Besides writing, she loves extra-hot lattes, fast cars and binge watching sci-fi movies.

You can find out more about the futuristic worlds she creates at sgbasu.com. She can also be reached at sg@sgbasu.com.

Made in the USA
Middletown, DE
19 November 2018